Hendrik Conscience

The Happiness of being Rich

Hendrik Conscience

The Happiness of being Rich

ISBN/EAN: 9783337300401

Printed in Europe, USA, Canada, Australia, Japan

Cover: Foto ©Andreas Hilbeck / pixelio.de

More available books at **www.hansebooks.com**

THE
Happiness of Being Rich.

By Hendrik Conscience.

AUTHOR OF "THE CURSE OF THE VILLAGE," "THE VILLAGE INN-KEEPER," "VEVA,"
"THE LION OF FLANDERS," "WOODEN CLARA," "COUNT HUGO OF CRAENHOVE,"
"THE POOR GENTLEMAN," "THE CONSCRIPT," "RICKETICKETACK,"
"BLIND ROSA," "THE MISER," "THE DEMON OF GOLD," &c.

Translated Expressly for this Edition.

BALTIMORE:
PUBLISHED BY JOHN MURPHY & CO.
182 BALTIMORE STREET.
PHILADELPHIA.....J. B. LIPPINCOTT & CO.
SOLD BY BOOKSELLERS GENERALLY.

1867.

Preface to the American Edition.

THE "HAPPINESS OF BEING RICH," like all the others Tales of this distinguished author, possesses a simple beauty that charms and delights the reader. Its scenes, deeply interesting in themselves, are rendered the more stricking and entertaining, by the under-current of humor, that flows beneath its style. Its purity and chasteness of sentiment, its freedom from every thing that could in the remotest degree offend the moral or religious sensibility or the most refined taste, or raise a scruple in the most fastidious mind, must and will commend it to universal favor.

HAPPINESS OF BEING RICH.

CHAPTER I.

"Oh, Katie dear, what heavenly weather it is to-day! Oh, the beautiful May-month! It feels to me like butter and milk—so balmy and so sweet!"

"Yes, Annemie, I don't know what ails my feet; they are itching to set off dancing by themselves. This first blessed sunny day makes me tremble all over with gladness; it seems to shine quite through me, bones and marrow and all."

"Only look how they are all pouring out of their houses to get a little of it. Now life begins to be snug and happy again; we can sit out in the street, and sing and chat and drink in the fresh air while we work."

"Yes, 'tis a blessing, isn't it, Trieny? after being shut up these four dreary, endless months in the house, like a poor bird in a cage."

"And scarcely able to draw our breath in the close smoky air of our rooms."

"And wear out our eyes in the gray murky winter days."

"Yes, and catch colds, and cough so that you feared that March would blow you away with him to another world."

"And forget that there is a sun in the sky; and count the days one after another, till the darling May brings light and warmth back again, for the poor man as well as for the rich lord—"

"Come, come, winter is gone by and forgotten; don't let us think of the old grumbler any more—

'Shepherds and shepherdesses gay
Sing and dance, for see—'tis May!'

Bring your frames a little nearer; we will sit here all four close together, else some kill-joy will come between us."

The young girls who were thus chanting, as they prattled, a feeling hymn of praise to the exhilarating May month, were sitting with many others in a long narrow street of the city of Antwerp.

The houses on either side of this little street were mean and small; they had each a little round-headed door at the entrance, and admitted the scanty daylight, yet further diminished in its transit through the green panes of their narrow windows.

One of the corner houses was distinguished from the others by its greater height and its new-fashioned window-frames. This was the grocer's corner; and although his customers were all of a very humble class, he had contrived to do very well, and at the end of a few years might be considered rich, in comparison with his humble neighbors.

Over the way stood an old house, which also boasted a first floor; but, for all that, its exterior was rather mean and dirty. Above the door was a sign-board, on which were painted two large letters, A. B. These signified that the house was occupied by a chimney-sweeper, or, as he was called in the Antwerp patois, a *Schouwveger*. This citizen ranked second in the street after the grocer, because his house was his own property.*

After him, in order of worldly consideration, followed a shoemaker, or rather a cobbler, who could not indeed boast of a house of his own, but yet contrived by industry to live without want and without care.

It was before the shoemaker's door that Katie and her three friends sat working; farther on in the street were many other damsels, who were also gathered into little groups, and continued their work amid reiterated exclamations and felicitations on the beauty of the weather.

Each of them had before her a square frame, on which was stretched a piece of net or woven lace; and on this they were embroidering, with needle and thread, flowers and foliage of every conceiv-

---

* In Antwerp the chimney-sweepers are reckoned among the lesser crafts, and are noted for their continual humor and mirthful disposition. The badge of their guild consists of the two letters, A. B.

able kind.   In Antwerp phrase, they were working
lace-stitch, in order that at the close of a long day
they might have earned a few sous, and so lighten
the burden of mother's housekeeping; also, in
good seasons, to buy a neat little frock, or a pretty
cap with gay-colored ribbons, for themselves.

Although these embroiderers belonged to the
lowest class of artisans, the cleanness and even ele
gance of their dress were very remarkable.   It is
an acknowledged fact that the Antwerp girls of
the lower classes are distinguished by an especial
cleanliness, and also by the becoming way in which
they arrange their dress; and, among them all, the
lace-stitch workers are very conspicuous.   How
can they help being always clean, when from
morning to night their hands are gliding over
snow-white net or lace?   If the least stain or soil
were to disfigure their work, they would be scolded
for their untidiness by the lace factors, be mulcted
of their pay, and refused further work.

You must not imagine, however, dear reader,
that this tidiness had its origin in necessity alone.
It may have been so at first, perhaps, but every one
knows the force of habit.   This remarkable cleanliness has now become quite a characteristic and
instinct of the lace-stitch workers; and if at any
time they are obliged to earn their daily bread by
labor of another kind, the same neatness and pro-
priety may be remarked in all they do.

Moreover, look at them well from head to foot:
their clothes are indeed very humble, and of com-

mon cotton; sometimes the color has partly disappeared; but how nicely washed—how neatly ironed out! not a speck, not a stain; it is as if they had seven Sundays in the week.

Are they pretty? Yes, and no. They are young, and that is something. Most of them might have been pretty too, for their features are fine and regular enough; but their cheeks are altogether so pale, their limbs so thin! Poor daughters of the people, luxury and wealth have hunted them out of all the open airy streets, built houses everywhere of which they could never pay the rent, and driven them back farther and farther into the dingy, dirty streets, in which neither burgher nor rich man cared to live. Drooping flowers, reared in dusky cellars and garrets, their blood is colorless, and consumption is the worm which lies gnawing at the root of the life of so many of them; and yet they are blithe, and they sing amid their everlasting toil!

Of the four girls who were sitting and working together before the shoemaker's door, there were two whose vital energies had not been impaired by lack of light and air and fitting nourishment. Their parents were in somewhat easier circumstances, and perhaps they had not, like their neighbors, lived generation after generation in the stifling, unwholesome cellars of this narrow street.

One of them was called Katie, and was the daughter of the shoemaker; the other was called

Annemie, and lived at the green-grocer's. The cheeks of both were ruddy with the fresh hue of youth, and their lips had not lost their exquisite coral-red. Katie had soft blue eyes and fair hair; Annemie looked as if she had Spanish blood in her veins, for her face was shadowed with a light brown, and her eyes and hair were black as jet.

While they were working quietly with their two companions, they saw at the end of the street a dame already advanced in years. She was coming toward them, and they followed her with their eyes until she disappeared at the little door of the chimney-sweeper's house. One of the girls then remarked:

"Dame Smet doesn't let the grass grow under her feet; she has got a new gown again, and a double-plaited cap—"

"Oh, Annemie, there you are again, always sneering and quizzing. What matter is it of ours what clothes other people wear, if they are able to pay for them?"

"Yes, Katie, that's very true; but for all that, you see, pride may have a good deal to do with it."

"Pride? Oh, she is such a good, kind creature!"

"Yes, yes; Dame Smet holds up her head as if my Lady Van Hoogenberg were her sister; and as she goes along in her grand gowns, she looks down on us as if we were not good enough to tie her shoes."

"You think so, Annemie; but I assure you it is not so. Everybody has her own ways. Dame

Smet is of a very good family. She has an aunt in Holland who is so rich, so rich! I don't know how many bags of gold she has—and, you see, when anybody comes of a good family it is in the blood, and you can't get rid of it again."

"Always with her prating about her family! What good does that do her? Everybody, even her own husband, laughs at her. I should be ashamed to make so much fuss about it; it is so absurd in the wife of a schouwveger."

Katie was not pleased with these taunts; she raised her voice, and said, in a sharper tone, as if she were a little out of humor—

"I don't know what concern it is of yours. Schouwveger or not, they live in their own house, and owe nobody any thing; they can pay their way, and needn't trouble themselves about the envy of their neighbors."

"It would be odd if *you* didn't like her," said another of the girls, with a smile; "she is Pauw's mother."

"Come, come, Katie, don't be vexed—it is only my way of talking," said Annemie. "Everybody bakes his own loaf as he likes it; and if he chooses to burn his fingers in the pan, that is his own look-out."

After a short pause, one of the girls asked, in a kindly tone—

"Tell us, now, Katie: I heard say yesterday—but I can't believe it—that you are going to be married."

M

With a heightened color on her cheeks, Katie
stammered out—

"Oh, these neighbors! Give them an inch, they
take an ell!"

"So, it is true, then?"

"Not quite: Master Smet has been joking about
it with my father."

"Ha, then the thing is half done. Well—good
luck to you, Katie!"

One of the other girls curled her lip with a kind
of disdain, and said—

"Ay, ay, Kate—to marry a chimney-sweep—a
fellow who is, six days in the week, as black as old
Nick himself! Why, if he were covered with gold
from head to foot, I wouldn't have him."

"That's because you can't get him!" muttered
Katie.

"I wouldn't have him either, though he is the
merriest lad in the whole quarter," remarked
another girl. "Sundays, when he is washed, he
is all very well; but in the week! you can't shake
hands with him but you must run off to the
pump; and when you talk to him, you have always that everlasting black phiz of his before your
eyes. Bless me! 'tis enough to frighten one out
of one's senses. When he laughs and shows his
white teeth, he cuts a face like a dog chewing
cayenne pepper—"

"What a wicked tongue you have!" interposed
the talkative Annemie. "Pauw is the best lad
you will find anywhere about; he sings such

merry songs, he dances and jumps—he is the life of the whole street. Everybody is glad when he comes by, for wherever he is there is laughter and merriment. And then look at him on Sundays, when he walks up and down with his blue coat, and tosses his head with his pretty cap on it! I say he is a very good-looking lad, and Katie is quite right to like him—especially if her father and mother don't object."

At this moment they heard at a distance the cry —*Aep, aep, aep!**—echoing merrily through the narrow street.

"Ah, there is Pauw, with his father!" exclaimed they all together, with a joyous laugh. "Ah, *Jan-Grap* and *Pauwken-Plezier!*"†

At one end of the street, some considerable distance from the group of girls, a man was seen approaching. He was about fifty years old, but in the full vigor of life, and walked with a light elastic step, and with his head quite upright. His like those of all the schouwvegers, were coarse, unbleached linen, and his body; he was covered and all—with soot. He seemed of temperament; for as he went along up a con-

---

* This is the customary cry of the they are bound to thrust their head and shout this cry three roughly done.

† Jan-Gladsome and

M

tinual laugh with the neighbors, and had a joke for everybody.

Five or six steps behind him came his son, Pauw; a sprightly youth, just on the verge of manhood. His face and clothes were black with soot; the whiteness of his eyes and teeth, and the living red of his lips, contrasted strikingly with his dusky features.

A sack filled with soot hung over his shoulder; in his right hand was a little brush, and, besides, a branch of whitethorn in full flower—the May-flower of the Antwerp people.

As he entered the street, humming a lively ditty, and making all kinds of astonishing leaps, his grimaces and gesticulations awakened the merriment of all the neighborhood.

"Vieze Breugel!"* said one.

"They may well call him Pauwken-Plezier," remarked another; "there is always laughing going ▓▓ he is."

"▓▓ old birds sing, so the young ones chirp. ▓▓ father will die laughing."

"▓▓ with the Antwerp chimney-sweepers ▓▓ the badge of their craft. A solemn schouwveger is more scarce than a lively under-taker."

"Well, that's what I like," said an old chair-maker, "they're quite in the right of it; they

---

* The name of a famous Flemish painter. His subjects were usually comic, and he was hence called *vieze*, funny or facetious.

don't neglect their work, and they pay everybody his own. Do well and live merry: you can't better that.

Annemie sprang up suddenly, and exclaimed—

"Listen! he's got a new song. Oh, isn't it a beautiful one? Where does he get them all from?"

"He makes them all himself," said Katie, with gratified pride.

"Dear me! is he such a scholar as that? I didn't know that."

"Yes; there isn't a single notice on the church door that he can't read: he has it all at his fingers' ends."

The young chimney-sweep had meanwhile come so near that they could distinguish what he was singing so lustily. It was a right merry ditty, and its light tripping melody was well adapted to the peculiar kind of dancing step which the Antwerp folk call a "flikker" and the French "un entrechat."

Pauwken-Plezier sang thus, with sundry odd grimaces by way of accompaniment:—

> " Schouwvegers gay, who live in A. B.,
>   Companions so jolly,
>   All frolic and folly,—
> Schouwvegers gay, who live in A. B.,
>   Come out, and sing us a glee.
>
> Your Schouwveger gay is a right merry fellow;
>   Though sooty his skin,
>   The wit's all within.

The blacker his phiz
The blither he is.
He climbs and he creeps—
He brushes and sweeps—
He sings and he leaps—
At each chimney he drinks till he's mellow.
Aep, aep, aep!
Light-hearted and free—
Always welcome is he!"

And as while he was singing he manifested a strong inclination to come very close to Katie, her companions uttered a loud scream, and held their hands spread over their frames to protect them from stain.

"No, Pauw; get along with you; be quiet, do; you will make our work dirty!" they shrieked.

But Pauw seemed to become suddenly more peaceful and quiet, under the inspiration of the sweet smile which Katie had bestowed on him at sight of the flowers. She well knew that the first gift of the fair May-month was destined for her; her blue eyes beamed with gentle gratitude, and they so touched the young schouwveger, that the song died away on his lips and the laugh from his countenance.

After a while, as though he could not be serious long together, he conquered his emotion, and said, laughingly—

"Katie, I have been roaming about the fields— that is to say, from village to village—and I have been singing *aep, aep, aep,* with all my might, in

opposition to the nightingales, until my throat is
as rough as a grater.   But I met out there a damsel, so beautiful, such a darling; and she was so
affectionate to me that I almost——Now, now,
don't be sulky, Katie.   The damsel asked me,
then, whether I had a liking for anybody?   I was
going to say *no*, but I didn't like to tell a lie; and
when I nodded my head to say *yes*, she asked me
what was the name of the girl I liked better than
anybody else.   'Ah,' said I, 'don't you know?
Ha, ha, 'tis a little lass like a rose, and her name
is Katie.'   'Ah, well,' says the young damsel,
'make my compliments to her, and give her these
flowers from me.'"

All the girls were staring at the chimney-sweep
with their mouths open, and a half-incredulous
smile on their faces.

"'And if you always love each other, in honor
and in virtue,' said she, then, 'I will make you
merry every year, and give you all kinds of flowers,
as many as you like.'"

"Who could it have been?" asked the palest
of the girls, in amazement.

"You know her well enough, all the time," said
Pauw, laughing.

"What is her name, then?"

"Her name is Mademoiselle de May."

"Mademoiselle de May? I know a Madame
de May, who lives round the corner at the drysalter's; but it can't be her."

"Oh! don't you see the rogue takes us all for

fools?" cried Annemic. "He means Mademoiselle de May-month!"

"Exactly so: I meant our old acquaintance!"
said Pauw, still laughing, as he gave the fragrant
branch of thorn to Katie, and said to another of
the girls—

"Trieny, will you have some? Oh, they smell
so nice!"

The girl reached out her hand, and Pauw struck
her gently with the branch.

"Oh my! you ugly old schouwveger!" exclaimed Trieny.

"No rose without a thorn," said Pauw, sport-
ively.

But Trieny was so vexed that she stood up, put
her arms akimbo, and assailed him thus:

"Oh, you black, sooty villain! what do you
think of yourself? You go roaming about doing
nothing, and think you may take any liberty. Go
and wash yourself, you dirty nigger. Your father
is at home already. Make haste, or you'll catch
the rod!"

"Look at the little dragoon, how well she rides
her horse!" said the young sweep, in a mocking
tone of voice. "You are not tongue-tied, anyhow, Trieny. Ill-temper doesn't become you—you
ought to have a nice pair of moustaches."

And with these words, he made a gesture as
though he were about to reach the face of the girl
with his black fingers; but all the group set on
him at once, and overwhelmed him with abuse:

"Hobgoblin! Ugly schouwveger! Soot-sack! Aep, aep, aep!" and sundry other curious appellations.

Pauw could not bear down the clamor, so he began to beat a retreat, shaking his head from side to side as if he would allow the shafts of their invectives to fly over his shoulders harmless. Then he shouted all at once—

"Holloa, my little darlings, I must just make an end of this, and then go and wash myself. Heads up! one, two, three!"

At these words he cut five or six capers in the air, and shook his soot-bag so vigorously that he diffused a dark cloud over the scene, singing the while—

"Sing and dance, Pauw, my boy—
For nobody can harm you."

All the girls raised their frames and ran off with cries of dismay, lest their work should be stained by the soot. While some were running and screaming, and others laughing and shouting, the schouwveger capered away toward the door of his house, shouting to them—

"Good-by, my dear little turtle-doves! *à tantôt.* I'll just go and put on my Sunday face!"

CHAPTER II.

THE little narrow street had been already for
half an hour wrapped in the shades of evening.
Mother Smet, the schouwveger's wife, was sitting
at a table, and was busy in darning the woollen
stockings of her Pauw, by the glimmering of a
small lamp. Her clothes were not simply clean—
they were more costly than her condition in life
would have indicated; for, although she was in her
own house, and would not probably go out again for
the evening, she wore a rose-colored jacket with
little flowers, a cloth gown trimmed with velvet,
and a cap white as snow, with stately wings.

Sad or irritating thoughts seemed to be passing
through her mind; for very often she would pause
in her work, and then her countenance would be
clouded with an expression of anger or vexation.

"That's the way they always cheat poor people
who happen to have any thing left them," she
muttered, at length. "They know how to mystify
it, and to draw it out, and put it off till the poor
legatee is dead, and then the rascals quietly put
the whole into their own pockets. It makes me
mad to think of it. Old Kobe the mason, in the
Winkel Street—he happened to have a hundred

thousand crowns left him; all was quite straight-forward—but they dragged him about backward and forward, from Herod to Pilate, so long, that he died of starvation in his little attic. Six months afterward the inheritance was shared between three or four great men, who didn't want it at all; and I suppose the best part of Kobe's share was left sticking to the fingers of those lawyers. But they shan't treat me so, I can tell them. If it cost me my last farthing, I'll see what has become of the legacy of my aunt in Holland—the precious thieves!"

At this moment her husband came down-stairs, blew out the lamp he had in his hand, set it down on a shelf, and then stood with his arms folded, looking with a smile on his amiable wife. The schouwveger's face was now washed quite clean; his clothes were such as were usually worn by the inferior burghers, whenever they went out of an evening to drink a pint of beer with their neighbors.

"I fancy I've pretty well served out the rats in the attic now," said he. "Only guess, Trees, what I have done?"

"Oh, let me alone," answered his wife, in a pet. "You have been serving out the rats these ten years past; but they serve us out the worst. Only leave any thing in the attic, and if 'tis only a soot-bag, they have gnawed it to pieces before morning."

"Well, how can I help it? Do you fancy I can

catch all the rats in the city? They are always
on the move, and they run along the drains and
gutters. They don't take a lease of a house; but
if they find themselves well off, there they stay.
I saw one morning, Trees, a black fellow with a
tail long enough to make a pair of garters of.
But, dame, your nose is out of joint to-day; you
don't ride your hobby easily. Always these sour
looks!"

"I look just as I like!"

"To be sure, to be sure — only so much the
worse that you do it on purpose. I have noticed
all day that you have got a thorn in your foot.
Something about lawyers, I fancy, or your aunt in
Holland, or legacies, bags of gold, and other
castles in the air?"

"'Tis no business of yours. What do *you* know
about it?"

"Well, Trees, listen once for all—quite seriously
and without laughing."

"Without laughing? You can't, you merry-
andrew, you!"

"Well, just listen. We have been married now
nearly five-and-twenty years; next year, come St.
John-in-the-oil, is our jubilee, our silver wedding-
feast.* All these years you have been running
about after lawyers, and tying up wills, and codi-

---

* May 6th, a feast in memory of St. John's being cast into a
cauldron of seething oil, and coming forth unhurt. The twenty-
fifth year of wedded life is the *silver* jubilee; the fiftieth, the
golden.

cils, and registers—and every month carrying ever
so many pretty francs to that little black man.
If all this money were in one heap, it would be a
snug little inheritance by itself; for there are a
good many mouths in five-and-twenty years.   Up
to now I have let you do what you liked; but now
every thing is so confoundedly dear.   Potatoes
are two francs the sack; meat is so dear that the
money I get for sweeping one chimney wouldn't
buy enough for us to point at—and bread, bread!"

"Yes, much you care what bread costs!" said his
wife, scornfully, "if only beer doesn't rise in price."

"Now, as long as there is enough, even if 'tis
something rather coarse, I shouldn't make a fuss
about it, mother dear.   A cheerful temper is as
good as bread.   But I'm getting out of my beat.
What I wanted to say to you is this: you lie
dreaming of *my aunts* and *my uncles*, and of all
sorts of miserable legacies you are going to get.
Stuff and nonsense, all the time!   And every day
you get worse and worse, Trees.   If you don't
leave off—you are growing old now—you will have
a screw loose in your head; and if you don't take
care, God only knows whether you won't find
yourself in the madhouse, with all your Dutch *my
aunts* and *my uncles*."

His wife stood up, and answered, with a smile of
derision on her lips: "Well, well, what one must
hear from one's own husband!.   Do you mean to
say that I am not of a good family?".

"Oh, no, my little wife; you come of a very

good family, I know—from the family of Jan everybody. Your father, of blessed memory, kept a
rag-shop, and sold all sorts of odds and ends, bits
of old iron, and copper, and lead; and people
thought he was rich—I suppose because he was
such an old screw; but when he died at last, no
money was forthcoming, and we got nothing but
our cottage. Well, that's quite enough. Your
niece goes about selling oranges, your venerable
aunt picks up old iron and bones, your uncle's son
is a fireman—most excellent, worthy, reputable
people, all of them; but that much fat drips from
their fingers—*that* isn't true."

"Who is talking of my family here in Belgium?
In Holland are Van den Bergs by the thousand."

"There are plenty more Janssens. These twenty
years you have been hunting up all the Van den
Bergs on the face of the earth, to see if any of them
belong to *our family*, and you have spent foolishly
I won't say how many crowns about it. Moon-
shine, every bit of it. A man sees just what he
likes to see. Go and stand on the wharf by the
Scheldt when there's a bit of breeze, and look at
the driving clouds. What will you see? A man
on horseback—Napoleon—a giant—a coach-and-
four—a dragon with seven heads? You have
only to wish—there it is before you. And so it
is with you. Trees dear, you have a regular
puppet-show in your brains."

The dame sat down again, and said, with desponding sadness on her every feature—

"It is wonderful how obstinate you are; and I was hoping you would go this afternoon to our lawyer's. The rogue, after keeping me waiting these two years, and getting hold of all my crowns —for wax, and paper, and letters, and I don't know what besides—has told me this very day that my family, large as it is, consists entirely of poor people. He has given me back all my letters and papers in a heap, and told me good-humoredly enough not to come to his house again."

"Well, that lawyer is a fine fellow. He might go on taking your money; but he doesn't want to fleece you, and he gives you good advice for nothing. There are not many such lawyers to be found—at least so says the song, for I don't know much about them myself; and if they had to live on my money, they would get precious little butter to their bread."

This colloquy seemed to have relieved Mother Smet of the vexation which had worried her all the day; so it was with a milder tone that she replied—

"Say what you like, I shall be rich yet before I'm laid in my grave. I am of a good family, and shall have some legacy. This very night I dreamed I found a lump of gold as big as the door-stone."

"Ha!" shouted the schouwveger, laughing; "then that's a sign you'll wait a long time. If you had dreamed of spider's webs, now—that betokens money—"

All at once they both heard a noise over their heads.

"Eh, what's that?" asked the chimney-sweeper.

"Don't you hear what it is?" said his wife, with a provoking smile; "'tis the rats come out into the attic again, and laughing at you for a fool. Much they care for the fine trick you have played them!"

"Well, that's wonderful!" growled Master Smet! "I filled up every hole and crevice just now with chalk and ground glass. I'll just go and see; perhaps I left one hole—but I don't hear them any more now."

"But, Smet," asked his wife, "suppose we were to become rich some fine day, what would you do?"

"For God's sake, Trees, don't worry me with all this stuff about being rich. We are not in want of any thing. Our Lord gives us our daily bread, and he gives me my pint of beer with my friends—what more could we wish for?"

"Yes; but if only you were rich, now?"

Her husband put his hand to his forehead, and answered, after a little consideration—

"What would I do? Let me see: I'd manage very well, you may be sure. In the first place, I would paint our house and our sign, and gild the A. B. Secondly, I'd buy four hams all at once, to make a good cheer in the winter. Thirdly—what would I do thirdly? Oh, I'd give four sacks of potatoes and six quarters of coal to the poor widow with her sick children, there round the corner. Fourthly, I'd buy a house for our Pauw; and the day he married Katie we would have such a wedding-feast that you should smell it all the way up to the Magpie hill."

"And is that all, now? that's well worth being rich for!"

"How do I know what I should do besides? But, once for all, I should live well, and make my friends live well too."

"And would you remain a chimney-sweep still?"

"Eh, what do you say?"

"Whether you would remain a chimney-sweep still?"

"Yes—that is to say, I should sweep chimneys for my own pleasure."

"Ha, ha, you stupid booby!" exclaimed his wife, bursting into a loud laugh.

"And what should I do else with my time?" asked Master Smet. "Do you think I should like to sit all day long in the public-house? Let us hear now, Trees, how *you* would manage matters if a treasure fell from the sky into our hands."

"Oh, I know how to manage much better. I am of a good family," said the wife, with a tone of exultation. "I should buy a large house in the Kipdorp, or on the Meir; I would have a coach and four horses, and a sledge for the winter. I would have my clothes of silk and velvet, with a muff and a boa—"

"What's that you say? A *boa*—what is that?"

N

"Oh, something to wear round the neck like fine ladies."

"Isn't that the tail of some wild beast?"

"Yes, indeed; that costs something!—and I would wear diamonds on my breast, in my ears, and on my fingers; and behind, my gown should have a long train, like the queens in the old comedies; and wherever I went, a footman should follow me—you know how I mean, with a yellow coat, and a gold band round his hat. And then I should come and walk through this street every day, to make the grocer's wife over the way burst with envy and spite—"

"Oh, leave off, leave off!" roared the chimney-sweeper, "or you'll make *me* burst with laughing. Don't you see my Lady Smet, the schouwveger's wife, walking the streets with a long train to her gown, with a fox's tail round her neck, and a great big canary-bird at her heels? If you are not talking like a fool now, Trees, then I knock under. You may put me in the madhouse at once; for one or other of us two has a bee in his bonnet. But only listen, what a row there is up-stairs: the rats are splitting with laughter at you, Trees."

"But what is the matter up in the attic? What a screaming and scampering! Just go and look, Smet. You'd better open all the holes again, for I think all the rats in the neighborhood have got together there since you took to playing them tricks."

The schouwveger rose from the table, lighted

his lamp, and took an old rusty sabre from behind the great chest.

"I'll let them see," said he; "but get out a few cents ready, Trees; for I want to go and get my pint of beer."

Mother Smet remained below and listened awhile to the noise that her husband made with his sabre, hewing and thrusting at the rats in the attic. But soon the noise ceased, and she fell into a deep reverie and dreamed of silken clothes, and diamond earrings, and footmen with gold bands round their hats.

She remained some time lost in contemplation of the happiness of being rich; a sweet smile illumined her countenance, and she kept nodding with her head as though her mind were giving reality to the images which her fancy shaped.

At last she heard the stairs creak beneath the heavy tread of her husband; she looked up in astonishment, for she saw no light on the staircase.

"Is your lamp gone out?" she asked.

•The schouwveger stalked down the stairs in silence, and came close to her with unsteady steps. He was trembling in every limb, and the perspiration stood in thick drops on his pale face.

His wife uttered a cry of terror; then she sprang up, and exclaimed—

"Good heavens! what has come over you? What have you seen?—a thief? a ghost?"

"Silence! silence! let me fetch my breath," murmured the chimney-sweeper, with hushed and stifled voice.

N   3*

"But what has happened, then?" shouted his wife; "you make me feel more dead than alive."

"Silence, I say! speak softer, Trees," mumbled her husband, as if paralyzed by fear. "Don't let anybody hear us."

He came closer to her, stooped his head over her shoulder, and whispered—

"Trees, Trees dear, your dream is come true— a treasure—such a great treasure!"

"Oh, poor, unhappy Smet!" shrieked his wife, in alarm; "he has lost his senses!"

"No, no; don't make any noise, or we are lost," said her excited husband, imploringly.

"But speak out, then; for goodness' sake, what has happened?"

"I have found a treasure, exactly as you dreamed."

"A lump of gold?"

"No, a bag of money—all silver and gold! Come, take the lamp; I'll let you see it."

His wife now grew pale in her turn, and trembled with astonishment. Now she began to believe that he was in earnest, and amid all her emotion a warm smile played about her lips. Following her husband, she said, beseechingly—

"O Smet, don't deceive me; if it isn't true, I shall die of vexation—"

"Hold your tongue, I tell you," muttered the schouwveger between his teeth, as he went up the stairs; "you will betray us."

"But how came you to find it?" asked his wife, with hushed voice.

Master Smet stood still, as though he wished to gratify the curiosity of his helpmate before showing her the treasure.

"You heard well enough, Trees," said he, "how I struck about on the floor with my sabre. When I got up-stairs there wasn't a rat to be seen, but those blows of mine made two jump out of a corner; they ran between my legs, and disappeared close to the centre-beam on which the roof is supported. I went up to the place with my lamp, but I found no opening nor crevice. After I had hunted in every hole and corner I went back to the great beam, for I couldn't conceive where the two rats had got to. Though I didn't see any hole, or crack even, in the beam, I struck it with my sabre—I don't know why, exactly. It sounded so hollow and made such a strange noise that I struck it harder and harder, thinking that the rats had taken up their abode inside. All of a sudden a little square plank started from the beam; and plump! down came something on my foot, so heavy that I was going to cry out with pain—"

"A lump of gold?"

"No, not exactly; a bag of money! It burst in falling, and all sorts of gold and silver coins rolled about the floor. I felt as if I had had a good blow from a hammer: the lamp fell out of my hand, I shook all over, and I was obliged to hold

by the wall to come down-stairs. Every thing
seemed to be turning round and round before my
eyes; I felt like a drunken man. Now come,
walk on the tips of your toes, and when you
speak, lower your voice as much as you can."

When they reached the attic, the chimney-
sweeper led his wife toward the centre-beam, and
let the light of the lamp fall on a large linen bag
which lay on the ground, with pieces of money all
around it.

Dame Smet fell on her knees with a suppressed
cry of joy, tore the bag open still farther, buried
her hands in the pieces of money, remained a short
time sunk in silent amazement, and then sprang
to her feet. She raised her hands above her head,
ran round and round the attic, and danced and
jumped, and at last shouted, with a loud cry—

"Oh! oh! I am bursting! I shall split! Let me
speak a bit! O blessed heavens! now we are rich,
rich as Jews!"

Full of terror, the schouwveger seized his wife
violently by the arm with one hand, laid the other
on her mouth, and growled angrily, and with a
threatening voice—

"You stupid, thoughtless fool! Be quiet, or I'll
pinch your arm black and blue. Do you want the
neighbors to know all about it?"

"Good heavens!" groaned his wife, quite terrified; "what's the matter now? You are making
a face as if you would kill me outright. How
money alters a man! All the five-and-twenty

years we have been married, I never saw your
eyes glare like that!"

The chimney-sweeper seemed surprised at his
own vehemence; he let go her arm, and continued
more calmly:

"No, no, Trees, I don't mean it; but, I beg you,
talk more softly, and don't make any noise.   Tell
me, where shall we put all this money?"

"Well, let us put it down-stairs in the great
chest, and lock it up."

"And suppose thieves were to come?"

"Why should they take it into their heads to
come just now?   The chest has stood there these
hundred years."

"Yes; but you can't be sure about it."

"You must put it somewhere, anyhow."

"Suppose I hide it under our bed in the straw?"

"Oh, one can see *you* are not used to money,
Smet.   Do you think rich people hide their money
in their beds?   Put it in the chest, I tell you.   If
you find a better place to-morrow, it will be time
enough to change our minds."

Taking the second lamp from the floor, the
chimney-sweeper said—

"Trees, you take the money in your apron.   I
will go down and lock the door, that nobody may
take us by surprise; and take care you don't let
the money chink as you carry it."

While his wife was descending the stairs with
a heavy freight of gold, Master Smet locked the
door, and drew the night-bolt; then he went to

the window, to the trap-door of the cellar, to the back door, and tried all the bolts and bars. Meanwhile his wife had locked all the treasure in the great chest, and she was already sitting at the table, staring into the air with heaving bosom, and lingering on the sweet contemplation of her wealth.

Her husband came close to her, stretched out his hand, and said, with a stern voice—

"The key!"

"The key?" exclaimed Dame Smet, in haughty amazement. "It shan't come to that in our old days—that you should keep the keys! I have kept them in all honor these five-and-twenty years. You would like, maybe, to squander the money in your schouwveger's club; but stop a bit: I keep the money-box!"

Master Smet shook his head impatiently.

"No," growled he; "it is to hinder you from wasting all the money. When we had but little, it didn't seem worth while to save; but now I'll take care that we lay by something for the time when we are old and infirm, else we may fall into poverty and misery before we die."

"Well, well, Smet, my lad, money doesn't do you any good," said the dame, with an angry, taunting voice. "Your talk like an old miser; you make a face like an undertaker—"

"Come, Trees, give me the key."

"The key? If I have to fight for it tooth and nail, I won't give it up.'

"Won't you take any thing out of the chest without my consent?"

"Well, that is to say, I won't go extravagantly to work; but that I shan't buy a few new clothes, and change my old earrings that I have worn so long for a rather better pair—are we not man and wife? If I were to listen to you, we should be poorer than we were before. If you don't get some enjoyment out of your money, you had better paint a quantity of ten-crown pieces on the wall; you would have the look of them all the same, and less trouble with them."

"You don't understand me, Trees. If you go now all at once and let out that we have plenty of money, by wearing clothes which are beyond our station in life, the neighbors will begin to gossip about it, and ask how we came by it.

"Well, and what matter if they do? The money belongs to me; my forefathers have lived in this house more than a hundred years. Besides, there was no money forthcoming after my father's sudden death—he hadn't time to say where he had hidden it. And what harm would it be if everybody knew that I had found my inheritance?"

"What harm, you senseless thing? If the thieves came to know that we have so much money, they would break into the house, steal the treasure, and murder us, perhaps."

"How timid the sight of this money has made you! I shouldn't know you again, Smet."

"Yes; and then consider that people wouldn't so easily believe us if we said that we had found the money. God grant we may not have the police on our shoulders; they may think it is stolen money. Then they would carry off the treasure to the police office, till the matter was properly inquired into. If the law once lays its hand on it, get it out again if you can! Alas! alas! we should be eased of our treasure, and perhaps die in misery, after all."

"Indeed," said the dame, anxiously, "I think you are right."

"O Trees, Trees dear, do be a little prudent for once; be a little more reserved, and don't tell anybody that we have become rich."

"Yes—if only I can be silent!" grumbled his wife, and she shrugged her shoulders. "I learned to talk from my mother, and she didn't let her tongue grow stiff for want of using."

"Good heavens! 'tis very unlucky!"

"If every rich man were like you, it would be unlucky indeed. But can't we let the neighbors know that we have had a legacy? I have talked long enough about it, I'm sure."

A smile overspread the face of the chimney-sweeper, and his eyes sparkled with joyful surprise. He remained a while in great meditation, and then said—

"That we have had a legacy—but then people would know that we have plenty of money in the house."

"Well?"

"And the thieves?"

"Oh, you have lost your wits."

"No; what do you think we will say?—that we shall soon get a legacy—that we have had tidings of your uncle in Holland—"

"Of my *aunt*—that will be better; and if I buy a bit of new clothes, or any little trifle, people will only think that we are using a little of our legacy beforehand."

"Well, you see, that will do; nobody will know that there is any money in the house, and everybody will allow that you are of a good family. But, Trees, you will be reasonable now, won't you, and spare our money a little?"

"Come, now, *our* money—you mean *my* money. I won't do more than our position requires."

"And we will tell Pauw the same story, or perhaps the lad might take a whim in his head, and turn spendthrift—"

"There—I hear him coming!" exclaimed the dame; "make haste and unbolt the door, or he will ask what is going on."

The chimmey-sweeper sprang up, unlocked the door, and sat down again with a calm countenance at the table, as if nothing at all had happened.

Outside the door, in the street, resounded the ditty—

> "Schouwvegers gay, who live in A. B.,
> Companions so jolly,
> All frolic and folly—"

4

and Pauw came singing and capering into the room.

Coming up to the table, he said, in a sprightly tone of voice, and talking very fast—

"Oh, oh, how we have laughed! If I had missed such a bit of fun, I should cry out, for my mouth is sore with laughing. Only think, they have made me captain of the birdcatchers' club!"*

"Come, come, don't make so much noise about it," grumbled his father.

"Oh, 'tisn't about that, father," joyously exclaimed Pauw. "You know, father, we had laid by some money to get a new flag made for our club? The fine painter in the Winkel Street— him they call Rubens, because he wears a broad hat and mustaches—well, now, he was to paint a great owl on the flag. Oh, oh, that was a clever notion! This evening, while we were sitting having a chat, all of a sudden he brought the new flag. We all jumped up, full of curiosity. Piet Kruls rolled the flag open; we looked at one another—and then we all burst out into such a terrible fit of laughter that three or four of us fell down on the ground, and the others were forced to hold their sides. But there was one who cut a

---

* There are at Antwerp clubs among the lower classes, the members of which lay by a little money regularly, in order to go bird-catching in the autumn with an owl.

very sour face, and this was the smith. Now guess what was painted on the flag."

"Oh, always at your childish pranks," said his mother. "What should there be on it?—why, an owl; I suppose."

"Yes, yes, an owl with a head as big as a child's of eight years old; but the fun of it was that the owl and the smith were as much alike as two drops of water. There was such a laughing and such a row! The smith wanted to drag out the painter by the hair of his head—the innkeeper wanted to turn the smith out of doors; we wanted to make it all up; three pint stoups were broken and two hats crushed—at last, all ended in a good hearty laugh, for Rubens promised to alter the owl. But what has come to you? You are not listening to me. Father is looking so solemn, and you, too, mother! You are not ill, I hope?"

"It is no time for jesting now," answered Dame Smet, in a very serious tone of voice. "Pauw, my lad, I want to tell you something: we are going to have a legacy!"

"Again?" shouted the youth, with mocking unbelief.

"This time it is true enough."

"I know this song well of old. Of course, from *my aunt* in Holland?"

"Yes, from my aunt in Holland."

"Come, come, mother, you have grown a little wiser now. It isn't true, father, is it?"

"It seems that it is true enough this time," answered Master Smet, with a confirmatory nod of his head.

"Ah, well," cried Pauw, laughing, "then I bespeak a new pair of breeches and a dozen shirt-collars, when the legacy comes!"

Both his parents held their peace, and looked grave and solemn. Pauw looked from one to the other in amazement, and grumbled:

"But, mother—but, father—you sit there quite in the dumps about the good news; tell me what you have heard."

"I have a headache," answered his father; "talking worries me. I will tell you to-morrow what we have reason to expect."

"And 'tis *my aunt's* legacy, which has been coming ever since—long before I came into the world?"

"Yes, yes; let us be quiet about it now."

Pauw shook his head doubtfully, and thought in himself—

"Something has turned up that they won't tell me. People who get legacies look more merry about it. Perhaps they have had some words; but I won't bother myself about that."

He took the second lamp, lighted it, and then said—

"To-morrow I must get up early, at four o'clock, to go and sweep three chimneys at the Château van Ranst. It is a good two hours' walk from here—so good-night."

"Pauw," said his mother, with a significant pride in her voice, "we are no longer schouw-vegers!—and when you go out to-morrow put on your Sunday clothes, do you hear?"

"Look now, mother: don't take it ill," said the lad, with a smile, "but that is going rather too far."

"And, anyhow, my lady's servant has been to say that you are not to go to the château to-morrow."

"That's quite another thing. Then I shall get a good long sleep. To-morrow the legacy will be flown away up the chimney, just like the other times. Good-night, mother; a pleasant sleep, father."

He went up-stairs with light and merry step, and hummed quite audibly as he went—

> "Schouwvegers gay, who live in A. B.,
>   Companions so jolly,
>   All frolic and folly—"

Master Smet and his wife remained sitting below at least two hours longer. Whatever efforts the dame made to induce her husband to betake himself to rest, it seemed that he could not make up his mind to leave the place where his treasure lay. He had already tried all the doors and bolts over and over again, when it struck midnight. Then, after one more anxious and protracted scrutiny, he followed his wife up the stairs; and still, as he went up, he turned his eyes, ten times at least, to the chest which contained his riches.

CHAPTER III.

THE nerves of the chimney-sweeper were so
much shaken by the finding of the treasure, that
the poor man, exhausted and tired as he was,
could not close his eyes. He turned from side to
side, stretched himself out and yawned, then
twisted his limbs about, and moaned with long
respirations. His heart beat violently and irregu-
larly; every now and then he felt as if a stream
of ice-cold water were being poured down his
back.

It happened at length that he wandered off into
a light doze; but at the moment when a man is
passing from waking to sleeping life, his nerves
are most quick and sensitive. The schouwveger
could not pass this moment; every time the
coming slumber broke the chain of his musings,
he sprang up in his bed and listened with terror
to some noise he fancied he had heard; and,
indeed, the rats in the attic were rushing up and
down, racing merrily one after another, or fighting,
with loud squeaking and crying—just as if they
were still in the house of a poor man, whose
slumbers are peaceful and sound, beyond reach of
disturbance.

It might be that he had at length, after long twist-ing and turning, got fairly off, for he snored very loud. Gradually his breathing became oppressed, and assumed a tone expressive of suffering, as though Master Smet were tormented by unseen spirits. The sweat of anguish stood in beads on his fore-head; all his limbs were violently contracted.

Suddenly the struggling words broke forth from his constricted breast, and he shouted, in a tone of distress—"No, no! it isn't true: I have no money! Oh! oh! let me go! let me go!"

His wife, roused from her sleep, seized her hus-band by the arm, gave him a vigorous shake, and exclaimed—

"Eh, Smet, what are you up to now? Is the nightmare astride of you? or are you out of your mind?"

The husband stared in horror all round the dusky room, and groaned and shuddered:

"Oh, dear me! where am I? Good heavens! I thought I was dead! Is that you, Trees?"

"Why, who on earth should it be? 'Tis all your snoring. You lie there wriggling and twisting like an eel on a gridiron. 'Tis easy enough to see that *you* are not used to money. It doesn't hinder me from sleeping, though I am so uncommonly glad; but, you see, I am of a good family."

"Oh, Trees!" moaned Master Smet, wiping the cold, clammy perspiration from his forehead, "oh, Trees, what I have suffered is not to be described! Only fancy: I was scarcely asleep, when something

o

came all of a sudden and sat down on my chest, and I felt as if it was trying to crush in my heart with its knees. It had its claws fastened in my neck, and squeezed my throat all up together. I couldn't make out at first what it was; but it was like a wild beast, with long black hair, and it had a great knife in its paw. It wanted to make me tell where the money was; and because I wouldn't, it gripped my throat, and was going to stick the knife into my heart. I felt I was dying; then my eyes seemed to open, and I screamed with terror when I saw what it was. Oh, Trees, I tremble now only to think of it: it was a thief, a murderer!"

"Come, come, leave off your boyish tricks!" said his wife, jestingly. "Why will you lie with your arm under your head? 'Tis that gives you the nightmare. 'Tis very late: just try to go asleep, and don't disturb me any more. Now, a good rest to you!"

In a few minutes Dame Smet was fast asleep again.

The luckless schouwveger was not so fortunate. He made no effort to fall asleep again, for his fright had taken away all inclination to rest. For full half an hour he lay, with his eyes wide open, staring at the darkness, and dreaming, though broad awake, of policemen and of thieves, so that at length he jumped out of bed and dressed, without making any noise.

Then he went, creeping along on the tips of his toes, to the place where he knew that a table stood, and felt over it with his hand, searching for something. A sigh of glad surprise escaped him, when he discovered his wife's pocket. He took out the key of the chest, and went down the stairs with slow and cautious steps.

When he reached the room below, he lighted a little lamp, went to the chest, opened it, gazed a while upon the money with an ecstatic smile, then locked the chest again, and sat down with his head on his hands and his elbows upon the table.

After a little silence, he began musing aloud:

"Ha! there it lies all safe. Ha! to be rich—to have money—what bliss! But, after all, it brings care and trouble with it, and it breaks one's night's rest, somehow. My wife has such grand notions; she wants to live in a big house, to wear rich clothes, to buy gold and diamonds! Pauw is young; he'll want to play the young gentleman, and spend a good deal; and so they'll make my poor money cut a pretty figure! It will melt away like snow in the sunshine—and at last— yes, at last—I shall have to lie upon straw in my old age, and perhaps go a-begging for my daily bread!"

This thought filled him with alarm; he pressed his hands forcibly against his head, and remained a moment staring, with a pale and bloodless face, into vacancy. Then he continued:

"Oh, what a misfortune to have a wife who can't keep her tongue still in her head! Early to-morrow morning, by daybreak at least, she will be

o

running about among her neighbors, and gossip-
ing and boasting that she is going to have a legacy.
Thousands won't be enough for her; she'll talk of
millions. Everybody will be full of it; all over
the city people will be talking about the schouwveger who has so suddenly become rich. The
thieves will be lurking about our house, and then
one of these fine nights they will be making off
with the treasure! I shall be poor again—poor
again! Oh, my God! what anxiety and misery
a rich man has to bear!"

After a little pause, he continued his musings:

"It is odd! I was as lively as a fish in the
water: men called me Jan-Grap, because I was so
full of fun. I knew nothing of sorrow or anxiety;
all that God sent me was dear to me; I sang,
I danced, I laughed—I thought there was no king
so happy as I was! And now? Now I shake
at the least puff of wind; I am afraid of myself
and of everybody else; I can't sleep—my heart is
thumping and knocking as if something terrible
was going to happen to me. I shall get better
soon; I shall get used to my riches. And if I
don't laugh or dance any more, 'tis quite natural:
a rich man must look grave and stately; it doesn't
become him to be laughing and joking. A body
can't have all sorts of happiness at once; and to
be rich is, after all, the greatest."

This last consideration seemed to infuse some
consolation into his heart; for he smiled, and
rubbed his hands, and mumbled some words of

gladness and content. In this mood, a new thought struck him, and he said, in a quieter and more gracious tone—

"When I was only a paltry craftsman, I helped the poor widow round the corner as far as I could. I felt so much pity for her unlucky little lambs of children, that I often wished to be rich that I might raise her out of her distress. Her husband—God rest his soul!—was my best friend; and I promised him on his death-bed that I would care for his children. Well, now I am rich. Won't I keep my promise? Ha, yes! to do good, to be tender-hearted, to help one's neighbor! Now—now I feel what a happiness it is to be rich! Well, what shall I give the poor widow? Fifty crowns? That's too much: they would spend it in extravagance; and if I go to work like that, my gold will soon come to an end. Who knows if I shouldn't make her ungrateful? Suppose, now, I give her ten crowns? I think that's enough. They have never seen so much money in their lives. It doesn't do to give poor people too much at once; they are not used to it, and they become greedy and lazy, when they come by it so easily. One mustn't encourage begging."

The schouwveger relapsed into silence, and seemed lost in meditation. Suddenly an expression of alarm and contempt spread itself over his countenance.

"But, Jan, my lad," said he, in a tone of disgust and reproof, "when you were poor and had

to save out of your day's wages, you gave them a
great deal more than that, by little and little!
Sometimes you put into the widow's hand the
cents you were going to spend on your daily glass
of beer; and, to make her happy, you stayed at
home all the evening without seeing your friends.
What a horrid thought! Can riches make a man
miserly and unpitying? Really, I feel something
that horrifies me. Oh, no, no! away with selfish-
ness! I will put aside the fifty crowns for the
widow, and allow her something regularly every
week out of it. Perhaps God will reward me, by
making my wealth sit easier on me, and delivering
me from the strange alarm which makes me shake
all over."

He rose up slowly, cast a scrutinizing look
round the room, and opened the chest. He stood
a while in silence, gazing on the heap of money,
the gold and silver pieces of which glittered before
his eyes like a cluster of stars. He then took out
seven ten-crown pieces, put them in his waistcoat-
pocket, and muttered to himself, in a joyous tone
of voice—

"I'll just put two more to them; the poor widow
is so very miserable, and it does me so much good
—the thought that I shall help the children of my
friend!"

Still gazing at his treasure, he fell into a silent
reverie, and appeared to be calculating in his mind
how much the heap of gold might amount to.

Suddenly, as if he had come to some conclusion,

he began to scrape together a large number of gold
pieces out of the treasure. When he had occupied
himself a while in this way, he went to the table,
and counted them over. "Fifty pieces," said he,
pondering deeply—"fifty pieces make five hundred
crowns; and five hundred Dutch crowns make
about a thousand and fifty francs. This sum I'll hide
away somewhere, where neither my wife nor my
son will be able to find it. If any misfortune
should happen to me, if thieves or gendarmes
should come, or if my wife should squander the
treasure, this would still remain for our Pauw;
and if he were to marry Katie, there would still
be something left to set them up in housekeeping,
and enable them to open a little shop."

He rolled up the money in a rag, went over to
the mantel-piece, drew forward a chair, and, standing on it, thrust his head as far as he could into
the chimney. He placed the pieces of money on
some projecting stones inside the chimney, and
felt secure that no one would think of searching
there for them. Then, jumping down into the
room again, he said, with a contented smile—

"Ha, now my mind is a little easier; now I shall
be able to sleep."

He was just about to blow out the lamp and go
up-stairs, when he suddenly checked himself, and
began to tremble with alarm. He fancied he heard
somebody trying to break open the window from
the outside; and, indeed, there was a sound as of
a man's hand touching the shutters.

The terrified schouwveger fixed his eyes upon
the window, and was so paralyzed by fear that the
lamp shook in his hand; when, to his great relief,
he heard the sound of steps retreating from the
window, and a hoarse voice singing in snatches—

"We were so jolly, and we tarried so long—
Ut, re, mi, fa, sol, la!"

"Oh, the drunken rascal!" growled Master
Smet. "He little thinks that he has half killed
me with fright—the noisy vagabond! The police
are fit for nothing! Anyhow, 'tis the rich people
that pay the police; why don't they at least take
care that rich people may be able to get a little
sleep?"

After listening some time longer at the window,
he blew the lamp out, crept softly up-stairs, put
the key of the chest again into his wife's pocket,
and lay down on the bed without undressing.

At last he fell asleep, and dozed for, it might
be, half an hour, without any other signs of rest-
lessness than an occasional contraction of his arms
and legs.

All of a sudden there was a loud noise in the
attic, as if something heavy had fallen on the floor.
The schouwveger started with terror from · his
sleep, jumped up from his bed in consternation,
and ran against a chair so violently that he over-
turned it, and it fell on the floor with a loud noise.

Thereupon his wife started up, and exclaimed
angrily—

"But, Smet, are you possessed, that you are playing such pranks in the dark? What's the matter with you now?"

"Oh, Trees, thieves!" groaned he, with choking voice. "Where is the sabre?"

"Come, come, you are dreaming again," said his wife, with a sneer. "Do you think the thieves can smell out money?"

"They are up in the attic; listen, listen!" whispered the schouwveger, pointing upward, with his hair on end, and pale as a sheet. And truly heavy steps were heard on the stairs, and soon some one knocked loudly at the door of the chamber.

Beside himself with fright, Master Smet threw up the window that looked out on the street, and screamed, with all his might—

"Help, help! thieves! murder!"

And in order to arouse his neighbors the more effectually, he added to his cry of distress the alarming words, "Fire! fire!"

He saw in the distance two persons who were running at full speed down the street, attracted by his screams.

A voice cried anxiously at the chamber-door—

"Father, father, open the door! Is the house on fire?"

"Oh, you fool!" muttered Dame Smet; "it is Pauw. "Let him in; you'll frighten the lad out of his wits."

"Where—where is the fire?" asked Pauw,

in consternation, as soon as the door was opened.

"It is nothing, nothing at all; I was only dreaming," stammered his father.

"Ha, I wish I knew what was going on!" said the lad, in perplexity. "It seems to me that our house has been haunted all night long; I haven't been able to sleep a wink. Overhead the rats are at work as if they were mad; down here I hear talking going on, chairs tumbling about, cries of murder and fire; and when I run down, with quaking heart, I find there is nothing at all the matter! Look you, father: don't be angry with me, but it seems to me as if you were busy playing Punch and Judy."

The schouwveger had sunk into a chair, and sobbed aloud, overcome by the fright he had experienced. The silence lasted a short time, during which Pauw stood awaiting an answer, with amazement increasing every moment.

"If I am not to know," he muttered, "I won't ask any more about it; but, father, what will the neighbors say? Heaven knows, you have roused up more than fifty of them out of their beds with your frightful cry of, 'Fire, fire!'"

"Your father was dreaming," said Dame Smet: "he can't get the legacy out of his head. Go to bed again, Pauw."

"What's that I hear now?" moaned the schouwveger, in fresh surprise.

The street seemed to shake beneath the rumbling of heavy wheels, coming at a great pace.

"Oh, 'tis the artillerymen going with their guns to the camp at Brasschaet," said Pauw; "but 'tis odd they should come through our street."

"What can it be?" exclaimed Dame Smet; "they are stopping at our door!"

Pauw opened the window, gave a look into the street, and, turning round into the room again, said, with a loud laugh—

"Well, here's a joke! 'tis the fire-brigade, with all their engines and pipes!"

There was a tremendous knocking at the door; every blow echoed distressingly through the heart of the schouwveger, who lay so crushed by his terror that he was unable to utter a word.

Pauw thrust his head out of the window again, and asked the men who were thundering with all their might at the door. "Holloa! what's the matter down there? Go about your business, and let folks sleep in peace!"

"Where is the fire?" exclaimed a voice.

"Where is the fire?" repeated Pauw. "Why, in the oven of oily Schram, the baker, to be sure; it's eight houses off, on the right-hand side of the way, close to the green-grocer's."

"I'll teach you how to cut your jokes up there!" said the sergeant of the fire-brigade. "Open the door this minute, or I'll break it open by force!"

"Don't put yourself in a passion, sergeant," said one of the firemen; "'tis Pauwken-Plezier;

5*

and if he tried to speak otherwise, the funny rogue couldn't do it for his life. Just let me manage him."

He went under the window, and called out—

"Pauwken, has there been any fire in the house?"

"Yes, there's a fire every day, an hour before dinner."

"No tricks, now, Pauwken. I was just coming through the street with my comrade, and your father was screaming, 'Fire, fire!' as if the whole parish was in flames."

"Yes, it was my father, talking in his sleep; he was only dreaming aloud!"

The sergeant now broke out in a towering passion:

"Come, come—I'll teach you to make fools of the police! Corporal, run and call the commissary; we will break open the door, and fine the insulting scoundrels."

The word commissary struck on the ear of the schouwveger; he started up, and cried out at the window, with a beseeching voice—

"Oh, firemen, my good fellows, have patience only a minute; I'll run down and open the door."

He left the chamber, followed by his son. As they descended the stairs, he groaned, with tremulous voice—

"Pauw, my boy, our house is bewitched! Oh, now, all the fire-brigade will come in. I am more dead than alive; I am quite ill with—"

"But, father, the firemen won't eat us all up, surely?" said the young man.

"Ah, you don't know, child, what your father will have to put up with!" moaned Master Smet, in a dejected tone. "Pauw, they will search the house all over, to see where the fire was. Since we can't help it now, you lead them round, for I can't stand on my legs."

The young man unlocked the door, while his father placed a chair close to the chest in which his treasure lay, and sank down on it, exhausted and breathless.

Five or six firemen then entered the room. The sergeant recognised the young wag, and seized him in a threatening manner by the shoulder, exclaiming—

"Ha, you young vagrant, you'll make sport of the fire-brigade, will you? How will you like to sit in the stocks, eh?"

Pauw sprang back, and cried, with a loud laugh—

"Look you, Mynheer Fireman, talk of the stocks as much as you like; but I am a free man; and if you dare to lay your hands on me, I'll teach you how to run, though I'm only a schouwveger, and don't wear a copper hat."

Seeing that Pauw was awkward flax to spin a good thread out of, the sergeant turned to Master Smet, and asked, angrily—

"Tell me, where's the fire?"

"Well, my good man, it is a mistake; there has been no fire here."

"Ha, you want to conceal it, to escape paying the fine.'"

"Oh, no; I thank you ten thousand times for all your trouble: there has been no fire here."

"And you frighten folks by shouting, 'Fire, fire!'"

"Yes, a man has odd dreams sometimes," stammered the schouwveger. "Just look at me, sergeant; I'm all of a shake; my nerves are out of order."

"Get up," said the sergeant, imperatively, "and let us see all the chimneys."

"I can't stand up," moaned the schouwveger, with a voice of entreaty. "My legs sink under me. Pauw, go round with Mynheer."

The sergeant made a sign to the corporal that he should follow the young man. Then he said to Master Smet—

"You sit there by your chest as if you were afraid we were going to steal your money!"

A shudder ran through all the limbs of the schouwveger, and a cold perspiration stood on his forehead.

"You shall pay dear for your jest," continued the sergeant; "you'll have to pay the fine."

"Is that all?" muttered the poor terror-stricken Smet. "Make me pay the fine two or three times over, if you like; only, for God's sake, get out of my house!"

Dame Smet, who had dressed herself in the mean time, now came into the room with a smiling countenance; and, as soon as she saw how the matter stood, she said in an easy tone to the chief of the fire-brigade—

"Sergeant, here's an odd affair. Don't be vexed about it; it was quite unintentional. I'll tell you all about it. You must know that we have had news of *my aunt* in Holland."

The schouwveger stretched out his hand with a gesture of entreaty to implore his wife to be silent; but she paid no attention to him, and went on:

"We are to have a legacy—I don't know how many thousand crowns. This news has come so suddenly on my husband that he has a fever in his brain—poor man! He has been dreaming that the house was on fire; but you see, my fine fellows, I don't wish you to have all your trouble for nothing. Drink a pint to our health, and be assured that we are very grateful to you for your promptitude and kindness."

With these words, she put a five-franc piece into his hand.

At this moment Pauw came down-stairs with the corporal. The latter advanced to the sergeant, brought his hand to his policeman's cap in military fashion, and said, in a pompous tone—

"Sergeant, there has been no fire in the house."

After sundry admonitions not to dream so loud another time, the fire-brigade left the abode of the schouwveger. His wife thereupon shut the door and locked it after them.

Raising his hands, the schouwveger said, with a sigh—

"Good heavens! if poor men only knew what a bother it is to be rich, they would never wish it. Here is a fine business!"

Dame Smet took him by the shoulder, and, pushing him toward the stairs, said, half in anger and half in scorn—

"Yes, a pretty mess you make of every thing. I ought to be vexed with you, but I pity your childish fancies. To-morrow we'll talk it all over. Go and sleep now, Zebedeus; and if you must dream of thieves and gendarmes, try to dream quietly. Money has made a fine fellow of you! Look at him, how he stands there like an idiot with the palsy!"

Without speaking a word, thoroughly crushed down and beside himself with the fright he had experienced, the poor schouwveger turned and slowly mounted the stairs to his bed-room.

CHAPTER IV.

THE morning after these noctural freaks, Dame Smet was on her legs betimes, and ran off to the corner shop to chatter and gossip about *my aunt* in Holland and the grand legacy they were going to have; and when the wife of the grocer ventured to express, with some scorn, her disbelief of Dame

Smet's oft-repeated story, the latter took out of
her pocket a handful of gold-pieces and laid them
on the counter, as vouchers for the truth of what
she said.   Thereupon the four or five dames who
were in the shop at the same time lifted up their
hands, and cried out in amazement, as if they had
been favored with a sight of all the treasures of
California.

Half an hour later, not a single person in the
neighborhood could plead ignorance of the fact
that Jan-Grap, the chimney-sweeper, had got a
legacy of three huge bags of gold.   Everybody
was making inquiries, and everybody was giving
answers; so that in a very short time Jan was
endowed by the liberality of his neighbors with
more than a hundred houses, and about twenty
ships at sea.

While Dame Smet was running all over the city
to visit the *magazins des modes*, and to give her
orders to a celebrated milliner, Pauw remained at
home, at her request, to await the appearance of
his father, who was somewhat indisposed by his
night's adventures.

And now Dame Smet had been about a quarter
of an hour at home; she was standing before the
looking-glass, admiring the brilliance of the huge
golden pendants she had suspended to her ears.

Pauw came down-stairs at the same moment,
and, in reply to a question of his mother's, he
said—

"Father isn't sick: he is out of sorts, and worn

P

out by the strange adventures of the night; but
he'll be down in less than an hour."

"Well, Pauw, just look at me," she exclaimed,
exultingly; "what do you think of these ear-rings?
Don't they suit me famously?"

The young man looked at his mother. The impression which the jewels made upon him could
not have been most favorable, for he shrugged
his shoulders, and replied, with a smile—

"I don't know, mother; but the ear-rings under
your plaited cap look as if they had lost their way
somehow."

"Now, now, wait a little; we will soon mend
that," said the dame. "Only wait a few days,
and your mother will come out in such style that
you shall see whether any *my lady* on the Meir
can compare with her! She will wear a *chapeau*
with feathers in it, a velvet *pélérine*, a purple silk
gown, and coffee-colored boots! And then she
will promenade up and down the street, with a
darling little parasol in her hand, so grand and so
stately that everybody shall see of what a good
family I am."

"Well, if there is no remedy for it," said Pauw,
sighing, and shaking his head, "for God's sake,
mother, go and live somewhere else; for such a
grand *my lady* in our little schouwveger's den will
be enough to make me swear awfully. I don't
feel inclined, mother, to be pointed at all my life
long and laughed at by everybody."

"Patience, patience, Pauw!" answered the happy

dame. "Your father won't change houses yet; he has his reasons. But only let us get the legacy, my boy! I've got such a beautiful house in my eye; that large *porte-cochère* on the St. James's market!"

"Do you know what I'm thinking, mother?" asked the young man, with a sad smile. "I'm thinking that all three of us are out of our senses; and as for the legacy, *if* I had ten crowns in my pocket, I wouldn't give them for the egg that isn't laid yet!"

"Ha! you wouldn't give ten crowns for it, eh?" exclaimed his mother. "Look, there's something like a proof for you, you unbelieving Thomas!"

Pauw sprang back in astonishment, and kept his dazzled eyes fixed on the handful of gold-pieces which his mother had taken out of her pocket and held before his face with an exulting laugh.

"Well, now, what do you say to that?" asked she. "Have you ever seen so much money in all your life before? Are these only clouds driven before the wind, as your father was saying?"

But the lad could not speak; he did nothing but stare at the gold-pieces.

"Have you lost your tongue?" said his mother, jestingly. "You stand there as if you had seen something uncanny!"

"Whew!" said Pauw, quite bewildered; "well I may, when you deal me such a stunning blow as that!"

P   6

"And this handful of gold is only a trifle compared with what we shall have."

"Well, mother, mother dear, are we then really rich?"

"Rich as Jews, Pauw!"

"Ha, ha! what a life we'll have! And Katie, poor thing, she'll be out of her senses with joy!"

He began then to cut some extraordinary capers, and sang out cheerily—

"Schouwvegers gay, who live in A.B.—"

But his mother placed her hand on his mouth and stopped his song, by saying, in a tone of rebuke—

"Fie, Pauw! singing a poor man's song—a low song! You must learn to behave like a lad who is of a good family."

"You are right, mother," stammered Pauw, in confusion; "I must make another little song—"

"No, no; no more singing or jumping about. A rich man must be grave and solemn."

This seemed to disconcert Pauw a little.

"Then mustn't I be merry any more?" he asked.

"Yes, yes, on the sly—when you are by yourself; and if you like to toss off a good flask when nobody sees you, the neighbors can't talk about it. That's the way rich men manage."

"When I'm by myself! Do you fancy, mother, I drink beer for the sake of drinking? Why, if I had no friends with me, I'd a great deal rather drink water."

"Beer, beer! rich men don't drink beer; they don't care for any thing but wine."

"And I don't like wine."

"Oh, you'll soon learn to like it. But the first thing you have to learn is to leave off your loose way of walking up the street, and your joking and quizzing."

"But mustn't I laugh any more, then?"

"In the street? No, certainly not. You must carry your head up in the air, hold yourself upright, and look stiff and stern."

"As if I was always vexed with everybody?"

"No, as if you were always abstracted and full of thought. There's nothing so vulgar as laughing and being merry."

"I don't quite fancy that. 'Tisn't worth while to be rich, if you can't have some pleasure out of your money!

Dame Smet sat down majestically at the table, as if she were going to say something very important and memorable.

"Pauw," said she, "just sit down a minute. I have something to say to you. You have sense enough to take my meaning. 'Like seeks like'—"

"Yes, and the devil ran away with the chimney-sweeper—at least, so the proverb goes on to say."

"Don't joke now, Pauw; and listen attentively to what I have to say. 'Like seeks like.' What would you say if you saw the son of a baron marry the daughter of a drysalter?"

"I should think it odd."

"Don't you think, Pauw, now we are so rich, that people would think it a disgrace if you were to marry a poor girl?"

The lad trembled with fear.

"Heavens! mother, what are you driving at?" be exclaimed, anxiously.

"Look now, Pauw. The shoemaker's Katie is a good and virtuous lass; I have not a word to say against her. And if we had remained poor people, you would have been married to her before the year is out;—but now—you see the whole city would laugh at us."

"Well, let them laugh, if they like," said Pauw, firmly. "I'd rather be a chimney-sweep with Katie than a baron with anybody else;—and look you, mother, you mustn't harp on this string, or I shall be as cross as a turnpike-gate."

Dame Smet put on a cunning expression, and said, in her blandest and most insinuating tone—

"But, Pauw, don't you think that Leocadie, in the corner shop there, over the way, is a comely lass? Black eyes—fine figure—always so well dressed—and such nice free manners; and there's heaps of money there, Pauw! If you would only set your cap at her, now—"

"Well, bless my soul!" exclaimed the lad. "Leocadie! that pale shrimp of a girl, with her ribbons and her curls! why, she's a walking perfumer's shop; I wouldn't have her if she was the king's own daughter. She is always *parlé*

fransé with those mincing rascals. No, no, I
won't have such a weathercock as that; when I
marry, I'll take care that my wife is really *my*
wife."

"What!" cried his mother, "are you not
ashamed to sit there and dare to take away the
good name of people who have four houses, all
their own property?"

"I don't want to take away any thing, mother;
only I won't hear you speak of that gilded grass-
hopper."

"Well, suppose you have no liking for Leocadie,
—you shan't marry Katie!"

"No?"

"No!"

"Well, then, I won't be a rich man—not I!"

"You will wait till we are in our proper position; and then some *mamsel* or other—"

"Some *mamsel?* I shouldn't know how to talk
to them. No, no; I won't have anybody but Katie!
Father has promised me already that he would
take care I married Katie; and he said, too,
that we should have such a merry, such a jolly
wedding."

"Father will change his mind when he is a
little used to being rich. You must forget Katie,
I tell you."

"I cannot forget her—I don't want to forget
her—and I won't forget her! Such a dear, good
child! she would die for her Pauw, if necessary—
and I am to break her heart and despise her, now

6*

we are rich! If I thought I could ever dream of
such a thing, I would dash my head against the
wall there."

"I don't wish you to see her any more," insisted his mother.

"Father has told me to go and see her this
morning, that she might not hear about our legacy
from anybody but me."

"Ha! then you are a little too late there; half
the city knows it already."

"But, mother," said Pauw, with a voice of
tender entreaty, "you must still have a heart?
Only think now, you have regarded Katie as your
daughter these five or six years past; you have
loved her as your own child. She loved you, too,
so much that we were often forced to laugh at her;
it was always 'Mother dear, this,' and 'Mother
dear, that;' the ground wasn't good enough for
you to set your foot on. When she was here to
keep you company, there was never a door opened
but Katie jumped up to shut it, for fear you should
catch cold; she watched your eyes to divine your
wishes—and no wonder: the dear child has no
mother of her own! When you were ill for more
than three months, I am sure she cried three
days at a stretch. Every morning she went to the
church to pray for you; she watched whole nights
long by your bedside; and when your illness became dangerous, she shed such floods of tears, and
was in such a state of grief, that the neighbors
hardly knew which to pity most, you or poor

Katie. I always loved Katie; but since I found out that she would have given her life for yours, I have loved her ten times more. I have quite a reverence for her; and all the *mamsels* in the city put together are not worth my Katie!—Oh, don't punish her for her goodness! She would break her heart and die—and you, mother, you would lay her in her coffin as the recompense of her love!"

The tears flowed fast from the young man's eyes as he spoke these words. Before he had half finished, his mother became so deeply affected that she had bent her head down to conceal her emotion. Wiping her face with her hands, she cried out—

"Pauw, lad, leave off, do; you would fetch tears out of a flint. Where did you get your words from? It is all quite true; the poor child would pine away. And she has never shown us any thing but pure, disinterested kindness and affection. It is a pity things should turn out so: she is not a girl fit for your station in life; but, rich or not rich, we are human beings still, and have hearts. Come, come, run off to Katie; fine clothes will help to set her off, and I will do my best to teach her good manners."

"Oh, mother, thanks, thanks!" shouted Pauw, intoxicated with joy. Do with me whatever you like. If I must mount spectacles, and wear yellow gloves, and set everybody laughing at me, I don't care, if only you won't vex Katie.'

He rose up, and was leaving the house.

"Pauw, hold your head up!" said his mother, authoritatively. "A rich man doesn't wear a cap like that; and here is a satin neckerchief for you, with red and blue stripes. Come to the glass, and I'll put it on for you."

With whatever vexation the young schouwveger might regard the gaudy colors of the satin, there was no help for it; so he meekly and patiently allowed the magnificent neckerchief to be tied round his neck; then he sprang out of the door, with a joyous farewell to his mother.

She called after him, reprovingly—

"Pauw, Pauw, no skipping and jumping; behave yourself soberly, as becomes your position in life!"

The sunny side of the street was, as usual, crowded with young lace-stitch workers, enticed from their close rooms by the beauty of the weather; and among them were most of the old dames of the street, basking in the sun and stitching away at their children's clothes.

To please his mother, Pauw had altered his whole bearing, and stalked majestically along, with his head erect, and a conscious stateliness about his whole person.

As soon as he came in sight of the girls, all ran up and looked at him with their eyes wide open, and with an expression of wonder and even of awe, as if a miracle had taken place before their faces.

This general observation annoyed Pauw exces-
sively. His face glowed with the crimson of shame;
and his head began to feel as if it were a pin-
cushion, and the girls were filling it with pins.
He made great efforts to vanquish his emotion;
and, going up to the girls who were sitting not far
from the shoemaker's door, he said, in an ap-
parently unembarrassed tone of voice—

"Why, Annemieken, what are you cutting such
a face of wonder as that for?   Do you fancy I am
an elephant or a shark?   Eh, you, yonder!"
shouted he to a group of dames who were staring
at him with their necks stretched out, "what's the
matter with you?"

No one laughed; there was a considerable inter-
val before even Annemie ventured to say to him,
with a deferential manner and a quiet voice—

"Mynheer Pauw, I wish you good luck; but I
am vexed, after all."

"Vexed!—why?"

"Why, the street will be so dull, now that the
merry Pauw is become a rich Mynheer, and is going to live on the Meir."

"Come, now, have done with your *mynheers;* I
am Pauwken-Plezier, just as I was before."

At this moment an aged man passed by, quite
bowed beneath the weight of years; he took off
his hat to Pauw, bared his head silvered with age,
and said, with an imploring smile on his countenance—

"Mynheer Smet, if you please, may I speak a

word with you? Do not take it amiss, I pray you, that I make so bold."

The young man began to blush to the very roots of his hair, and exclaimed, impatiently—

"Come, Father Mieris, you are cutting your jokes at me, too, are you? Give me your hand; how goes your health?"

The old man smiled gratefully at the warm pressure of Pauw's hand.

"It is too great an honor, Mynheer Smet," continued he; "I have a small request to make of you. My daughter Susanna, you know her well."

"Know her? Of course I do; a good and tidy lass."

"She is an ironing girl, Mynheer Pauw, and works as hard and as well as the best. I am come to ask your good word with my lady your mother, that she might not forget us, and let us earn a few sous; for times are hard now, and bread is so—"

Pauw was quite bewildered by this time; his head began to turn round and round.

"Yes, yes; all right!" said he, interrupting the old man; "I will do it. But let me alone with all your *mynheers* and *my ladies.* The whole quarter will be in the madhouse soon, I think."

Terrified at this outburst, the old man shrank timidly back, and went away with sad and downcast eyes.

"Katie is shoe-binding, I suppose?" inquired Pauw of the girls.

"Yes, Katie, poor creature!" sighed Annemie,

with a look of deep compassion, "she is most to be pitied. If she survive it, it will be a great blessing."

The schouwveger became pale as death, and stepped toward the shoemaker's door, without further remark.

He found the girl sitting near the little window that looked out into the street. She had her apron before her eyes, and was sobbing aloud.

Pauw seized her hand and uttered a cry of painful surprise; but the, sorrowing girl gently and sadly withdrew it, covered her face more completely, while deep sobs of anguish burst from her breast.

"Katie, Katie," cried the young man, in despair, "what are you in such trouble about? what is it? Speak to me, oh, speak!"

The girl uncovered her face and raised her reddened eyes to her lover's face with an expression of unutterable grief and dejection, and said, imploringly—

"Oh, Pauw, you mustn't take it to heart; I know it isn't your fault. You would never have had the cruelty to give your poor Katie her death-blow."

"But, for God's sake, what has happened?" shouted the youth.

"I will bear my bitter lot; and even if I pine and die, I shall never blame you, Pauw; and I shall even pray that God may give you a wife who will love you as well as I do!"

"Ha, ha! 'tis the fear of that!" cried the young man, quite relieved. "Cheer up, then, Katie; between us there is no change: you are deceiving yourself."

The maiden looked at him with a smile of deep misery, and said—

"Oh, Pauw, I am far too lowly a girl to dare to lift my eyes up to such as you. You are of a high family, and my father is only an honorable crafts-man."

The young man stamped his foot on the ground with angry impetuosity.

"Who has put such notions into your head, Katie? the wicked tongues of the neighbors, I suppose? Katie, do you listen to their envious talk?"

"No, no," sobbed the girl; "your mother scoffed at us in the shop over the way, and said that no cobbler's daughter should ever come into her family. You must be obedient, Pauw. Leave me alone with my sorrow; it will pass away."

And, with a fresh flood of quiet tears, she added: "When I am laid in the churchyard— when you go out to walk sometimes, and you see in the distance the trees of the Stuivenberg,* think sometimes of our love, Pauw, and say in your heart—'There lies Katie, who died so young because she loved me too well.'"

---

* A cemetery in the suburbs of the city.

Pauw had covered his eyes with his hands, and trembled with emotion.

"Katie," said he, quickly, and in a tone of deep sorrow, "you are piercing my heart by your injustice. Were my father a king, you should be my little wife still! My mother herself does not wish it otherwise."

. "She feels too bitter a contempt for us, Pauw."

"Well, well; but you know riches blind people for a moment. My mother has sent me to you; she loves you as much as ever; and it isn't ten minutes ago she said to me, 'Rich or not rich, Katie shall be my daughter.'"

The girl began to tremble in every limb; she looked at the youth with glistening eyes and heaving bosom.

"Oh, heavens! good heavens!" she exclaimed; "Dame Smet, you will be my mother still! The death I saw floating before my eyes will flee away again; and I may be once more happy in the world! Pauw, Pauw, oh, don't deceive me!"

At this moment the shoemaker entered the room. He had evidently just risen up from his work, for he had his awl in his hand. He bent a severe look on the young man, and said—

"Mynheer Smet, I am surprised that you dare to come into our house again. We are poor indeed and humble, but we are honorable, and every man is a king in his own house. It is, perhaps, no fault of yours; but that matters not. Go hence —forget where we live—or else—"

7

"Oh, father dear, don't be angry!" cried the young girl; "it is not as you think."

"Your parents act by reason and by rule," said the shoemaker, with a bitter sneer. "As long as we were fellows in the same guild, all was right enough; but now that they have got a legacy of ever so many sacks of gold, now it would be a great disgrace that you, Pauw, should marry the daughter of a mere nobody—the daughter of a poor cobbler! But the cobbler has a heart in his body, for all that; and he will not allow you henceforth to cast an eye on his daughter. Go to the great streets, and seek there a wife suitable to your condition!"

"Master Dries, you are cruel and unjust," said the young man, stammering with vexation and alarm. "My mother sends me to you to crave your forgiveness for some thoughtless words she has uttered. It was not seriously meant, and she begs you to be kind enough to forget what has passed."

"No, no," answered the shoemaker; "that won't do. She has scorned us openly, before everybody. You, Pauw, must keep away from my house. We are not rich; but yet, look you, it shall never be said that we let ourselves be trampled under foot by anybody."

"And if my mother were to come herself, and confessed to you that she did not mean what she said?"

"Look you, now, that would look like something," muttered Master Dries.

"Well, now, she will come; I'll go and fetch her."

"I saw her go out just this minute," remarked the shoemaker.

"Then I'll go home as soon as she comes back, and ask her to come and speak to you."

"No, no, not so, Pauw; you shall not stay here. And I won't have you come unless your mother is with you. The neighbors are standing in a crowd at our door. Come, come; if all is as you say, every thing will come right of itself; but now, I must beg you, Pauw, to leave my house, and go home."

The young man turned toward the door, and said to the girl, as he took leave, "Katie, Katie, don't be alarmed; keep a good heart; all will go right enough. I shall be back again directly with my mother."

When Pauw entered his home, he found his father sitting at the table. The poor man was pale, and looked very desponding; his eyes, wearied with his unwonted and involuntary vigil, were dull and restless.

"Pauw, why are you so red in the face?" he asked, in some surprise.

"Why, father," was the answer, "I have been to Katie; she was sitting sobbing and crying so, that I could have broken my heart to see her. The shoemaker wanted to turn me out of doors;

Q

but we have come to an understanding. Are you
ill, father? You seem to me to look so pale; shall
I run for the doctor?"

"No, no, it is gone now; it was nothing but a
disturbance of the nerves. And what was the
cause of Katie's sorrow? what made the shoemaker so angry with you?"

"Why, I don't exactly know; mother has said
in the shop yonder that Katie was not good
enough to enter our family; and thereupon—you
can easily fancy how—the shoemaker got on the
high horse. But he is off again by this time; and
when mother comes home, I will go with her to
the shoemaker's, and set all straight."

"Your mother! your mother!" said the schouwveger, with a deep sigh, "she will make us all
miserable. She can't restrain her pride, and chats
and gossips as if we had ever so many thousand
crowns coming to us."

"Three sacks of gold, father. When I was
coming just now from the shoemaker's, Annemie,
there at the green-grocer's, asked me if it was true
that we had, over and above the sacks of gold,
I don't know how many houses and ships on the
sea."

"Good heavens!" said the schouwveger, sadly;
"'tis very unlucky! With all this chattering and
prating of your mother, we shall never have a
moment's peace again. All the thieves and vaga-
bonds of the city will be lurking about the house.
God only knows how many plots will be con-

trived to break in here at the first opportunity, and rob us—murder us, perhaps!"

"Yes, indeed, father; that is very likely. It seems the whole city is standing in groups, discussing our wonderful legacy."

"Wonderful legacy?" repeated the schouwveger, scratching his head in desperation. "Ah, Pauw, there is not near so much as they say."

"The neighbors say it is at least three sacks of gold," said Pauw, laughing.

"The neighbors are out of their senses."

"Well, father, wasn't there at least one single sack of gold?"

"No, no; only a moderate burgher's fortune: enough to live quietly on with care and economy."

"Whom am I to believe? Mother talks of a great house with a *porte-cochère* on St. James's Place; of hats with feathers; of maid-servants and footmen; and of so many other things, that I really thought she had found Fortunatus's purse, and we were going to live in a mountain of gold."

"Your mother will bring us to lie on straw again," cried Master Smet, with bitterness and wrath. "But wait—I'll let her see that I am master here. And if I once get off my hook, I'll trample her hat and feathers under my feet, and tear all her silk clothes to pieces; and if she won't dress as she ought to do, I'll turn her out of doors. Yes, yes, don't look at me so, Pauw; I'll turn her out of doors! And you, too; what's that round your neck, you prodigal?"

Q   7*

"Oh, bless me! I had forgotten all about it," sighed Pauw, tearing the satin neckerchief from his throat. "Mother made me put it on; but the fewer colored rags I have on my body the better I shall be pleased."

The young man now started backward, keeping his eye fixed with gloomy surprise upon his father, who had again stooped down with his head on his hands, as though exhausted by fatigue, and was looking vacantly at the table.

After a while Pauw said, half angrily—

"I wish the legacy was—I know where! We were not born for riches; we don't take kindly to them. Would you believe, father, that I'd rather remain poor than pass my life like this?"

"Oh, my child, don't wish for poverty," said his father, with a sigh. "If your mother does not behave more sensibly, we shall soon be cast down again into the depth of misery and want. Perhaps they already stand threatening at our door!"

The tone of his father's voice was so singularly harsh and melancholy, that the young man looked at him with a kind of terror, and exclaimed, with painful anxiety—

"But, father, you are ill—very ill!"

"There's nothing the matter with me; I am only a little bit tired," was the faint reply.

"How is it possible? Can the money have thus changed us all? Your eyes are cloudy, your face is pale, your voice is quite changed from what it was; all is so slow and so languid now, father.

Ah, we were always so happy, and so merry; you used to sing from morning till night; every word you uttered was so funny that no one could help laughing. I feel sure that money is a foe to joy; for now and then I find my own head falling on my breast, and something—I don't know what— begins to gnaw at my heart."

"Yes, my boy," muttered the schouwveger, "there is indeed some truth in what you say; but yet to be rich is a great advantage."

"So it seems!" said Pauw, bitterly. "Since there has been talk of this confounded legacy, I have heard nothing but grumbling and lamentation. I begin to fear that people will soon call us Jan-Sorg (*careworn*) and Pauwken-Verdriet (*fretful*)."

"It's all your mother's fault," said Master Smet, in a tone of vexation; "her love of extravagance is what worries me. Only fancy, Pauw, she is gone off to look out for a maid-servant; and she has made up her mind not to have any one who has not lived with some *my lady!* I set myself against it, and was very angry; but get an idea out of your mother's head if you can! Strange people in my house? Why, I shall never sleep in peace again!"

"But why are you so afraid of everybody, father? If we had got the legacy, and if there was a great treasure, here in the house, I could understand it; but now—"

The front door was opened at this moment, and

a personage entered, whose appearance cut short
Pauw's sentence.

It was a young footboy, with a golden band
round his hat, and clothed in an old livery coat,
which hung about his body like a sack, and the
tails of which reached down to his heels. The
fellow had sandy hair, and a coarse lumpish face,
which betokened an unwonted stolidity.

At his entrance, he stared round the room quite
bewildered, and muttered, half aloud, to himself—
"The people in the city are determined to take
me for a fool! I'm regularly taken in; but anyhow I'll ask—"

"Well, now, what do you mean by this?" cried
Pauw.

"It is only, you see, my lad," answered the
footboy, "I am not where I ought to be. The
girls in the street there have taken me in. I
wanted to find my lady the schouwveger's wife,
who has, all at once, got so many bags of gold
and ships at sea."

"Well, that is here," answered Pauw.

"Here, here, in this house?" stammered the
footboy. "A *my lady* here? It can't be."

"If you won't believe it, begone as quick as you
can, and leave us in peace."

The schouwveger shook his head in anxious
thought, but spoke not a word; he kept his eye
fixed on the table, with a smile of bitter contempt
on his face.

"If it is here," said the boy to Pauw, "then

I may as well say what I've come about. You must know I live with my lady van Steen. She took me from running after the cows, and said I should live the life of a lord; but you wouldn't believe how I have been treated. It is nothing but a thump here and a kick there! Since I jammed the tail of her half-starved lapdog in the door, and set the window-curtains on fire by accident, she can't bear to set her eyes on me. I hear nothing but—'donkey, booby, country lout,' and—but you have known all about it, I dare say —the words rich people use. I have heard say that your lady wanted a footman, to stand behind her carriage, and carry her muff or her prayer-book. Besides, I can turn my hand to any thing— horses especially I can groom and take care of. You are, I suppose, the stable-boy; and the old fellow there is, perhaps, the coachman of my lady. Put in a good word for me, both of you; we shall understand one another very well, and contrive to live a jolly life."

Pauw looked at his father with a merry laugh; but the schouwveger broke out into a furious passion. He sprang up, clenched his fist, and roared to the footboy—

"Get out of my house, you shameless scoundrel! Quick! look sharp! or I'll knock you into the middle of the street!"

The poor footboy, seeing him prepare to execute his threat, slunk out at the door in consternation, and muttered—

"Now, now, don't bite me. I haven't done you any harm. These great city lords—I believe they all have a screw loose in their heads."

And when he had said these words, he shut the door quickly, and ran away as fast as his legs would carry him.

The door opened again very soon. It was Dame Smet, who strode into the room, darting angry and threatening looks at her husband and at her son.

"Pauw," growled the schouwveger, pale with anger, "I am going up-stairs, for I feel I can't lay hands on a woman; if I stay here, I shall do something—"

And, so saying, he went grumbling up the stairs.

"What's going on now?" asked the dame, in a haughty tone of voice.

"Oh, nothing at all, mother," answered the youth. "A stupid lout of a boy came here to offer himself as servant, and we have sent him about his business. If you must hire a servant, you may as well get one who is fit to be seen."

"Oh, is that all?" muttered she. "I thought, by your father's looks, that something dreadful had happened again."

Pauw took her hand, and asked, with a voice of earnest entreaty—

"Mother, may I ask you something, before you take off your cloak?"

"Yes, to be sure, child; any thing you like."

"Oh, mother, I have been to Katie. If you had seen her, you would have burst into tears; the poor lamb was almost dying. She implores you just to go to her house, and tell her that you are not angry with her; and I, knowing your dear kind heart, mother—I promised you would come. Come, mother, come!"

"You wheedling rogue, you!" said the dame, with a smile, "who could refuse you any thing?"

Pauw went to the foot of the stairs, and shouted out, "Father, I am going with mother close by to the shoemaker's. We shall be back again in a minute."

And, with a joyous countenance, he led his mother out of the house.

CHAPTER V.

As if the treasure had been only an envious sprite who had assumed this form to torment the poor schouwveger, his house, once so happy, was changed into a hell of gloom and sadness and discord.

My lady Smet—for so she insisted on being called by the neighbors—had for some days been in delighted possession of her new clothes and of her silk *chapeau*. From head to foot she was covered with velvet and with satin; she wore gold in her ears, gold round her neck, gold on her bosom, and gold on both her hands.

Thus apparelled and adorned, quite like a genuine *my lady*, she roamed all over the city, and felt not the slightest annoyance when she saw that everybody stopped and stared at her as she passed—in amazement or in amusement,—and that many pointed at her with their fingers.

This universal attention was, on the contrary, a source of great delight to her, and flattered her pride extremely. She fancied that the boys said one to another, "There goes the wife of the schouwveger who has so suddenly become rich as a Jew."

And all this pointing and whispering was far from appearing to her a rebuke; she thought the passers-by were admiring the stateliness of her bearing and the grace with which she walked. She read in the eyes of every one she met, "Look, there is my lady Smet! What a fine woman! what dignity! One can see at once that she is of a good family!"

Indeed, had not the fame of her wonderful legacy made her known all over the city, no one would have distinguished her from a real *my lady*—except, perhaps, that the suddenly-raised schouwveger's lady was covered with clothes and golden ornaments, like the figures in the window of a *magasin des modes;* that she carried her head somewhat stiffly, and turned it so slowly and so perseveringly in all directions, just as though it were set on a pivot; that she had great broad feet, and took great strides like a man; that her face was very red, and that she seemed to ask every one she met, "Well, now, what do you think of that? I hope you see now that *my lady* Smet is of a good family!"

She liked best of all to walk round the Meir and the Egg-market, where the most splendid and fashionable shops were to be found. There she would make some little purchases, and gossip by the hour with the shopkeeper's wife and daughters, all about *my aunt* in Holland, and about her intention to take a house, and furnish it as grandly and as richly as that of the first nobleman of the land.

She inquired daily and of everybody whether they knew of a good housemaid, or a good cook, of a coachman, a stable-boy, or a footman. She asked everybody's opinion which was the most stylish color to choose for the horses she was going to buy; and gave it as her opinion that the Meir was not a healthy situation to live in, because there was a large drain under the street. Therefore she had determined to take a house with a *porte-cochère* on the St. James's market-place; and since the owner would not sell it, she meant to rent it until some good opportunity of buying presented itself.

After having in the course of her ramble sufficiently exhibited herself to the wondering city, she returned homeward; and she took care never to walk twice on the same side of her own street, so that all the neighbors might have the benefit of seeing and admiring her.

On her former acquaintance she would bestow a

8

cold smile of condescending benevolence. She called some of the dames by their Christian names; promised them all her protection and good graces; and this she did so haughtily that the poor people who were the objects of her civility felt their hearts overflow with gall at sight of the proud and supercilious upstart.

The schouwveger was about the unhappiest man on the face of the earth. He knew well that the treasure was not inexhaustible, and grumbled from morning till night at the extravagance of his wife. She avenged herself by calling him a hunks, a miser, a hair-splitter, and averred that any one could see that *he* didn't come of a good family.

Besides, the money was *hers*, and not *his*, and she might do what she liked with it. She had no notion of living like people who never saw more than one crown at a time; and if he chose to bite a farthing into quarters, and sit wearing himself out like an old miser, she would let him see that she knew how rich people spent their money.

Then the schouwveger would go into a violent passion, and insist on having the key of the chest; and then *my lady*, forgetting the proprieties of her station, would put her arms akimbo, and overwhelm her hapless spouse with such a flood of abuse and threatenings, that he was invariably obliged to beat a retreat, and creep up-stairs, with tears in his eyes, to grumble by himself.

Sometimes matters went still farther; on one occasion their strife had ended in blows. The schouwveger had, after considerable provocation, laid his hand somewhat uncivilly on the shoulder of his disdainful spouse; but my lady Smet, irritated by this unwarrantable liberty, had sprung at him like a wild cat, and ploughed his face with her nails.

There the matter ended; but both husband and wife looked so spitefully at each other, and were so furious, that there remained no hope of reconciliation. For several days not a word passed between them; or if by chance one of them addressed a question to the other, the answer was a snarl or a vicious growl.

Dame Smet insisted on taking the great house on the St. James's market. Her husband talked very loud, and declared that he didn't mean to move. This disagreement led to violent and prolonged quarrels, and already the dame had declared more than once that she would go off to her lawyer, and petition the supreme court for a divorce.

Pauw, the merry lad, had lost all his mirth and energy. The everlasting disputes and quarrels of his parents had broken his spirit quite; for, though he talked in an off-hand way, and turned everything into ridicule, he had a tender and affectionate heart.

No joke escaped him now; and when he made a faint attempt to say something lively, it was quite a failure; he couldn't help it — but there was always an undertone of bitterness and sadness in his voice.

Whenever he was alone with his father, he used every effort to comfort him and to soothe his irritated spirit. When he was with his mother, he tried with gentle and loving words to make her see that his father was perhaps a little too overbearing, but that his carefulness and frugality might easily be excused.

Poor Pauw's efforts were all in vain. No sooner did his parents meet again than the niggardliness of the one came in collision with the extravagance of the other, and the contest was renewed with increased vigor and bitterness.

In the young man's heart was another point of anguish and depression. His mother had, it is true, abandoned her intention of separating him from Katie; but she had never ceased to impress on the poor child a sense of her great inferiority, and to inflict the deepest wounds possible on the self-respect of the shoemaker.

When Katie came to see her, she insisted on instructing her how to walk, and how to stand; how she must speak, and how she ought to salute her neighbors; how she ought to carry her head, and how she must turn out her toes.

The sorrowful maiden, sustained by her deep affection, submitted with exemplary meekness to the whims and follies of her future mother; she even seemed gratified whenever Dame Smet impressed upon her what a favor, what an honor, they conferred on her in admitting her into so good a family.

In the shop and in the neighborhood, whenever the matter was talked over, *my lady* Smet recounted her generosity and true nobleness of soul, and instanced how she had consented, out of mere good-nature, to the marriage of her son with the daughter of a—shoemaker.   She had even ventured to say to Katie's father that it was a very great honor for him to become a member of so distinguished a family.

The depreciating remarks of Dame Smet were a constant worry to the shoemaker.   He did not conceal his vexation from Pauw, to whom he muttered his doubts how the marriage would turn out, and declared that he would put a stop to it, if Dame Smet persisted in treating his daughter like a beggar-maid, who was just tolerated out of charity.

The shoemaker, although only a poor artisan, had a pride of his own ; and he would assuredly have long since refused to admit Pauw into his house, had not both the lad and his father said all kinds of soothing words to him, and implored his forgiveness with tears in their eyes.   But though he postponed the final decision, there remained an increasing bitterness in his heart, and he no longer regarded Pauw with a favorable eye.

These untoward occurrences began to alarm the two young people not unfrequently.   When Pauw was seated by Katie's side, the tears would flow silently down their cheeks.

Eight days had already passed since the discovery

of the treasure; the schouwveger had not once left his house, except to go to church on Sunday.

It was now Monday, and the evening was falling in; there had been already a violent quarrel—with this difference, however, that this time it was followed by an apparent reconciliation.

-Dame Smet availed herself of the propitious moment to convince her husband that he did wrong in sitting at home all day long, and that it would be better, both for his health and for his understanding, that he should go about a bit among the neighbors.

Pauw promised, at his father's request, that he would not leave the house unprotected; and so the schouwveger allowed himself to be persuaded to go out and drink a pint of beer with his friends.

His wife had expended much eloquence in the attempt to convince him that he ought not to go into a public-house, but into a *café* in the Cathedral Close, or on the Meir, and that he ought to begin to drink wine. But, being now in a good humor, she agreed at length that her husband might take a turn outside the city, toward the Dyke, just as he used to do.

When the schouwveger came to the Dyke, and found himself among his old friends, some time was occupied in congratulations; but as soon as they had placed themselves round the table to have a game at cards, these remarks ceased of themselves, and the schouwveger felt as comfortable

and as merry as before he became rich. How
cheering the sound of the voices of his friends!
What real affection and heartfelt peace in every
one of their words! How soft and inspiriting the
taste of his customary beer! What a relish there
was in his pipe! How enchantingly the smoke
rose in clouds above their heads!

Master Smet felt himself in another world, and
for some hours forgot all about his treasure—forgot
even his wife. He found again some of his former
jokes, and more than once caused his friends a
hearty laugh.

The clock of the public-house was striking ten,
when the schouwveger, astonished that the time
had passed so quickly, rose and said that he must
return home.

They tried to keep him. There was in another
public-house a match going on between two
butchers, which should eat most hard eggs; and
they wanted to sit it out.

Master Smet, who had already remained much
too late, through forgetfulness, shook hands with
his friends, and assured them that he would come
and keep them company some evenings every
week, just as he did before.

It was quite half an hour's walk from the Dyke
to the gate of the city, and the road was very
lonely.

The night was dark; but, as the schouwveger
had gone this road a hundred times, he walked on
without fear.

R

He felt very glad that he had seen his friends: his heart beat more lightly, and in the darkness a gentle smile played about his lips; for he was thinking, as he walked, how many pleasant evenings he should spend there on the Dyke, among his old friends, now that spring was come again. And now he had reached the outskirts of the city, and was walking under some high trees, without thought or apprehension of danger.

All at once a suppressed cry of terror escaped him. A man sprang from behind a tree, and held a pistol to the breast of the trembling schouwveger.

"If you scream or cry, you're a dead man," said the robber, gruffly.

"What—what do you want of me?" stammered poor Smet, half dead with fright.

"Your money or your life!" said the other, with a threatening gesture.

"There—there is all I have: a five-franc piece and a few cents."

"You are telling a lie; you've had a legacy. I'll have your money, or I'll put this through you!" roared the thief, whistling at the same time, as if to make a signal to some one at a little distance.

Thereupon two other rogues came running from among the underwood; one of them thrust a handkerchief into the schouwveger's mouth, and the other tripped him up on the grass.

They felt in all his pockets; they took away his silver watch; they tore his blouse, and thumped and kicked him cruelly. The poor man could make no noise, and felt, with unutterable agony, that they were about to murder him.

Frightful words rang in his ears:—

"Kill him, the rascal! he has cheated us, the thief!"

Whether it was that the robbers heard the sound of approaching footsteps, or that they were convinced that nothing more was to be got out of their victim, they gave the schouwveger a few parting blows with their fists, then added a few vigorous kicks, and threw him into a thicket; they then ran away at full speed, and were soon lost in the gloom.

Master Smet remained for some time quite stunned; but, as he had received no dangerous wound, he came round, rose up, and ran as fast as he could along the road to the gate of the city.

He thought of running into the first house he came to, and asking for assistance to pursue the thieves; but then he felt that this was of no use; and, besides, he feared that the whole city, and especially the commissary of police, would begin to meddle with his affairs.

Like a true miser—for such he had now become—he preferred digesting his bitter chagrin as best he could, to drawing universal attention toward himself, and perhaps having to answer the inquiries of the police concerning his treasure.

So he walked on, with beating heart, and shak-

R

ing all over with pain and terror, through the city gate, and along the street toward his dwelling; and as he walked, melancholy musings on the immense advantages of being rich forced their way into his mind, and more than once he cursed the treasure which had occasioned him such continual grief, so much contention and vexation, so much soreness of heart, and such peril. He thought sadly of his former life, of his poverty, and of his happiness and his uninterrupted mirth; and sometimes he even asked himself whether it would not be better for him to divide the treasure among his needy neighbors. But all these speculations vanished at the touch of the demon of gold who held him captive in his grasp; and his heart clung with fiery eagerness to his beloved treasure.

Thus wavering between despair, terror, and covetousness, he reached his house, and sank into a chair with a heavy sigh. His wife and his son tended him with affectionate care, and listened with a shudder to the account he gave of his adventures. The schouwveger could not close his eyes all that night. No sooner did he begin to doze, than he dreamt of thieves and murderers; and, besides, he felt the smart of the blows which he had received on his head and shoulders, and —elsewhere.

CHAPTER VI.

THE next morning a rumor ran through the street that Dame Smet had not had any legacy, and had no chance of any. The lawyer who had been worried for years in searching out all her genealogy had said that the Smets had no relatives in Holland, and consequently could receive no legacy.

The mysterious secrecy of the schouwveger gave credit to this rumor. The envy and bitterness of the neighbors, excited by Dame Smet's haughtiness, gladly seized it as a foundation and pretext for all kinds of conjectures and surmises as to the origin of the sudden wealth of the schouwveger.

Their suspicions were still further confirmed when they noticed that three or four police agents were wandering up and down the street without any apparent object; they noticed, too, that every now and then they looked askance at the schouwveger's house, like ravenous birds who have caught scent of their prey, without knowing precisely where to pounce upon it.

Then a story got abroad that just a week before—the very night before the news of the legacy reached them—there had been a robbery at a

money-changer's in the city, and that the thieves
had made off with a large quantity of silver and
gold. Nobody ventured to say directly that the
schouwveger was likely to rob any one of a stiver;
but then, money couldn't drop from the clouds;
and, anyhow, the Smets must know where they
got it from.

Pauw was sitting in the shoemaker's house, at
Katie's side; she was working at her embroidery,
and had great difficulty in restraining the tears
which would trickle down upon her work in spite
of her efforts. The young man's head hung down,
and he was silent and moody; his countenance
indicated violent and unwonted emotion; his forehead glowed at intervals with indignation and
anger; then his features would relax into an expression of utter despondency, or a cold shudder
would thrill through his whole frame. He could
not help knowing what fearful suspicions were
hinted in the neighborhood about his father; and
he was evidently lost in melancholy musing, and
trembled beneath the crushing blow of shame.

The maiden, compassionating his distress, made
every effort to suppress her own sorrow, and tried
to comfort him by saying, with a sigh—

"Pauw, don't give way to low spirits. Men have
evil tongues. Don't fret about it. What matters
the gossip of the neighbors, if your parents can
show where they got their money?"

"The money!" muttered the youth between his
teeth. "Ah, Katie dear, it is the money that

makes us all so wretched! My father is growing
as thin as a skeleton; he will fall ill and waste
away. My mother, poor thing! I dare not say
what I think about her. She has her five senses
still; but what will come of her? There are times
when I tremble for her reason! And your father
is so cross to me! And I can't blame him; he
has to submit to so much humiliation. Ah, Katie,
Katie, what will happen now, when up and down
the street they say things about my poor, innocent
father which make my hair stand on end with
terror and shame. Oh, Katie dear, I shake all
over; I am full of fear. There is something that
tells me we shall be separated; that there is
nothing before either of us, all our life long, but
misery and sorrow."

The maiden hid her face in her hands.

"Katie," continued Pauw, with a deeper emotion
in his voice, "this morning I went quietly to the
church, and prayed more than an hour before the
crucifix. I besought God, with tears, that he would
be so merciful as to make us poor again!"

The girl raised her head, and said, with tears in
her eyes—

"Pauw, you must not give way to all these
gloomy fancies. There are so many rich people;
do you think they are all miserable?"

"I don't know, Katie; but to us, at least, money
is poison and gall. Since that wretched day we
have had nothing but quarrelling, anger, terror,
and suffering. My father was nearly murdered

9

yesterday. Yesterday, the knife of the murderer;
to-day, the knife of slander and calumny! Oh, it
is dreadful! to hear that my father has been rob-
bing—that he is a thief—and not to be able to find
out the serpent who first cast this venom on my
father's name!"

At this moment the shoemaker entered the
house. His face was pale, and betokened great
discomposure; he looked as if something had
frightened him out of his senses.

"Katie," said he, speaking very fast, "go up
into your room; leave me alone with Pauw; but
first bolt the street-door."

The girl uttered a shriek of anguish, and raised
her hands imploringly to her father, as if to depre-
cate some cruel sentence; but an imperative
glance of his eye, and the repetition of his com
mand, compelled her to obey. She left the room,
covering her eyes with her hands.

The shoemaker placed himself in front of Pauw,
and asked, with a voice of emotion—"Pauw, where
did your father get the money that your mother is
spending by handfuls?"

The young schouwveger looked at him in amazement, but did not answer quickly enough to please
the shoemaker.

"Speak, speak! where does the money come
from? It is for your own good I ask."

"My mother got it as a legacy," stammered
Pauw.

"Has the legacy come already?"

"No, not yet."

"Where does the money come from, then?"

"They have got some in advance, I suppose."

"From whom? From where?"

"I don't know any thing about it."

"You don't know any thing about it, poor fellow! My poor friend Smet, what will come to him next? Oh, God!"

"But what is the matter?" cried Pauw, in evident terror. "You are quite ruffled. What has happened? I am shaking like a reed; you are killing me with agony!"

The shoemaker took him by the hand, led him away from the window, and said, in a mysterious and melancholy tone—

"Pauw, I was sent for just now to measure one of the servants of the commissary of police for a pair of shoes. It was only a trick: the commissary himself wanted to speak to me. He asked me a great many questions about your father, about the legacy, about the explanations your mother has given the neighbors as to the source of the money she displays everywhere in such abundance. I cannot tell you what the commissary said to me confidentially; but I am very sorry for your father, who was always my dear friend; and if he has done wrong, I shall always lament his unhappy fate."

Pauw stood looking into the shoemaker's eye with a vacant stare, and shivering as if he had the ague.

."I pity *you*, Pauw, and my poor Katie, too; for she is not to blame—nor you either, Pauw."

"For God's sake, speak! What has happened?" sobbed the youth, quite beside himself.

"Pauw," said the shoemaker, lowering his voice to a whisper, "tell your father to be off out of the way as soon as he can; for the officers are coming to apprehend him."

"To apprehend him!" exclaimed Pauw, with an expression of indignation and pride on his face; "to apprehend my father! Ha! ha! how absurd!"

"Believe me, Pauw," repeated the shoemaker, in a tone of entreaty; "take my advice, or your father is a lost man!"

Then, putting his mouth close to Pauw's ear, he whispered, almost inaudibly—

"A large sum of money has been stolen from a money-changer's; they suspect your father of being, at least, an accomplice."

Pauw shuddered violently, and stared at the shoemaker with fixed and glassy eyes.

"What!" he exclaimed, "can you believe such a slander? Do you think it possible that my father is a thief?"

"No, no; but if he cannot show how he came by the money, how can he exculpate himself?"

"He *will* show all about it. How can you doubt it?"

"So much the better. I have asked him several times, but there was always something about him that was not clear and straightforward. Do just as you like, Pauw; but you see, until the thing is sifted to the bottom, you must keep away from here. Katie has nothing but her good name. You must not rob her of this, her only riches."

A shriek of despair and of agony broke from the young man's heart. He sprang up, and exclaimed—

"Ha! I'll know all about it; I *will* know all about it."

And, with these words, he ran out of the room into the street.

When he entered his own dwelling, he found his father alone, sitting on a chair.

He locked the door and bolted it, and said, with eager haste—

"Father, father dear, don't be angry with me; but I can't keep it any longer: I *must* know all about it."

The schouwveger gazed at him in astonishment.

"Father, tell me—oh, tell me now—where does the money come from that my mother is showing to everybody?"

"We have received it as a legacy," was the reply.

"No, no, the legacy hasn't come yet; you have got in advance, haven't you? You have borrowed it here in the city upon the legacy you are going to receive?"

"Well, yes. Why do you trouble yourself about it?"

"Where have you borrowed it? where?" repeated the young man, with feverish impatience.

"But, Pauw, what has come to you?" cried the schouwveger, in a severe tone of voice; "you impudent fellow! to cross-examine your father as if you were his judge!"

This word affected the youth deeply.

"I will, I must, I am determined to know!" he screamed.

Master Smet shook his head sadly, and said, in a desponding tone—

"Pauw, you are asking me something that I cannot tell you now."

"That you cannot tell me!" said the trembling youth, with a deep sigh. "Oh, good heavens!"

"What is the matter with you, Pauw?"

"Father, father," exclaimed he, "a large sum of money has been stolen from a money-changer's; people suspect you of being an accomplice in the robbery!"

The schouwveger was struck with dismay, but he exerted himself to hide his discomposure.

"It is only a slander of some envious people," stammered he; "don't disturb yourself about them."

"Alas, alas! the gendarmes are coming, father, to apprehend you!"

A death-like paleness overspread the schouwveger's face; he uttered a low moan, and began to tremble on his chair.

The sudden emotion of his father filled Pauw

with alarm. He clasped his hands in an attitude of supplication, and implored his father—

"For God's sake, father, speak! Where—from whom—did you or mother get this money?"

The schouwveger continued silent.

"Alas!" said Pauw, mournfully, "can it be true? Can it be that my father dares not declare where the money came from? Alas! I shall die of shame!"

At this imputation, made by his own son, the schouwveger covered his eyes with his hands, and began to weep bitterly. The tears which escaped from between his fingers and fell to the ground so affected the poor young man that he uttered a loud cry of anguish and sorrow.

He threw his arm round his father's neck, kissed him tenderly on the forehead, and said, with tears—

"Oh, forgive me, father; I am *so* miserable!"

"Accused by my own son!" sobbed the schouw- veger. "Oh, God! how have I deserved this?"

"No, no," said Pauw, beseechingly; "but I am compelled to hear you accused, and I cannot vin- dicate you. People ask me where you got the money. Oh, father dear, do tell me!"

"I cannot—I must not," repeated Master Smet.

And observing that these words drove the color again from his son's cheeks, he added—

"But be sure of one thing: your father is an honest man."

"And the gendarmes, father? will you not tell them?" cried Pauw, trembling violently.

The schouwveger rose up, as though he wished to avoid further questioning; and pointing with his finger to the door, he said, in a tone of command—

"Pauw, go away; leave me alone; I command you."

"Oh, father, father!" cried the youth, wringing his hands in despair.

"Obey me at once—go away!" repeated the schouwveger, with evident irritation.

Pauw raised his hands above his head, and fled from his home with a shriek of terror and suspicion.

For about half an hour the schouwveger was all alone. His eyes were fixed and still, but he saw nothing; he was pondering all the vexation and misery the treasure had brought with it, and how his house was changed into a hell of unrest and of suffering. During this gloomy reverie there arose and grew in his heart a feeling of bitter hatred toward the fatal money which had robbed him of the peace and of the happiness of his life. The demon of avarice tried, indeed, to crush the insurrection of his better soul; but the thought that his own son believed him guilty, and the indescribable terror which the approaching visit of the gendarmes excited in him, lent him sufficient strength to resist its fascinations.

He resolved, at length, when the officers of justice entered his house, to explain every thing frankly; and even if they took away the treasure

with them, in God's name, then, he would be a
schouwveger again, as he had been before.

This resolution made him feel lighter at heart,
and even cheered him so much that he felt he
should again be merry and open-hearted, as Jan-
Grap had been in days past.

When Dame Smet returned from her morning
promenade, her husband repeated what Pauw had
said; and he added that he had made a firm and
unchangeable resolve to declare every thing openly, and even to surrender the treasure into the
hands of justice, if it were demanded.

His wife knew much better than he did what
rumors were in circulation about them, and what
they had to fear. She first of all poured a torrent
of abuse on the poor shoemaker, who, she said,
had gone to the commissary, and, out of sheer
envy, had set all this mischief afloat. Then she
made her husband repeat again what Pauw had
said, and answered, with a scornful laugh—

"But, Smet, what a blockhead you have grown!
The word 'gendarme' makes your heart shrink
within you. Have you committed theft or robbery? What can they do to you?

"'Tis all the same; I won't tell a lie before the
judge."

"No—tell it all right out, you booby! You
know well enough that when justice lays its hand
on any thing, there is no getting it out again. The
lawyers and the men from Brussels would make
fine fun with your money! They would have a

good laugh at the stupid bird that let itself be plucked so easily !"

"Say what you like, I will conceal nothing —and, secondly, this money, d'ye see, begins to choke me terribly: I wish it were now in the mountain where they say all this cursed gold grows."

Dame Smet flew into a violent rage, stuck her hands in her sides, and snarled—

"Ha! that's the tune you're going to sing, is it? Well, we'll see! 'Tis *my* money; *your* forefathers never had a stiver more than enough to keep them from dying of starvation day by day. What! you will give up the inheritance of my father to the lawyers? Quick—speak out! do you abide by this stupid resolution?"

Her husband, disconcerted by the fierce glare of her eyes, and by the fear that matters would not end with words only, did not dare to say *yes;* but still he nodded his head affirmatively.

"You thief!" cried she. "You will rob me of my gold, and give it away to strange people who have nothing to do with it, will you? Well, then, I will not remain a moment more the wife of such a simple fool. I'll be off at once to an advocate. I'll be divorced from you—the law allows it— and then you may be poor, if you like, and sweep chimneys; for meanness runs in your blood—low rascal that you are !"

"But, wife dear," sobbed the affrighted schouw-veger, pale as death, "only listen to sound reason."

"What sound reason? You have never had a grain of sound reason in all your family. Speak, I tell you—will you behave as I wish, or not?"

Her husband remained silent.

"Well," growled she, "I'll make very short work of it. I'll be off with my money, and you shall never set eyes on me more."

And as the schouwveger remained silent, and with his head hung dejectedly down, she flamed forth into more violent anger. She rushed to the chest, and began in good earnest to fill her pockets with money, and packed up a great deal more in a table-cloth, shaking all the time with passion, and muttering—

"Well—you shall see! Stay you here, Jannoodle—and let the gendarmes fit a halter to your neck at their ease! Fare you well—*au revoir!* I'm off for America in the first ship—ay, farther than that too—so that I may never hear of you again!"

The schouwveger knew well enough that his wife had not the slightest intention of putting these formidable threats into execution. Still, he shuddered at the thought that she would be running round the neighborhood with all this money about her, and making herself a laughing-stock to everybody; so he made a spring at the door, drew the bolt, and put the key in his pocket.

His wife, finding herself thus a prisoner, burst out into wild invectives, and used every exertion

8

to take the key from her husband by main force.
And this domestic conflict raged on until the
schouwveger lost courage and gave way, pro-
mising faithfully to do just what his wife wished
him to do.

It was then resolved that, in case the officers of
justice made their appearance, they should affirm
that the money came to them from the father of
Dame Smet, and that they had kept it secret thus
long. It would not do to speak of an advance
upon the expected legacy, because they could not
say who made the advance. The rest of the
money they would hide again in the beam where
they had found it, and they would place the little
plank which covered the opening in its former
position.

Dame Smet overwhelmed her hapless husband
with threats of what she would do to him if he
should betray, by word or look, where the money
lay hidden.

When the treasure had been carried into the
attic, to the very last piece of gold, Dame Smet
tried to raise her husband's spirits and to rekindle
in him the love of riches; but the schouwveger
was like a man stunned at the thought of appearing in a court of justice. This seemed to him
a disgraceful, a punishable matter; and now he
trembled, in all sincerity, like a thief who is
caught in the fact. He heard nothing of his wife's
glowing descriptions; but the slightest sound in
the street affected his nerves so much that he

seemed at each moment to hear the awful voice of the gendarmes or the police.

And in the intervals of his paroxysms of terror, he muttered, in a tone of the deepest anguish—

"Cursed treasure! devilish money!"

———— • ————

CHAPTER VII.

An hour later the little narrow street was full of groups of people, who were discussing in amazement some unusual occurrence.

While they were chatting, every one's eyes were anxiously fixed on the house of the schouwveger, at the door of which a gendarme kept guard.

Katie was leaning against the wall of her house, with her apron at her eyes, and weeping bitterly. Some girls who stood round her seemed to participate in her grief; and Annemie, especially, made many attempts to console her; but she herself could hardly restrain the tears which stood glistening in her eyes.

The largest group was posted immediately opposite the schouwveger's door, and there were exchanged all kinds of edifying reflections and observations on this strange event.

"Serves her right!" muttered a fish-wife; "this will teach her to *my lady* herself—the upstart

s   10

minx, with her silk bonnet and her satin gown!
Now she can tell all the honest folk in the house
of correction what a good family she comes of.
And if she wants to show herself off, the scaffold
is quite large enough!"

"Yes, she comes of a great family—doesn't
she?" said another, with a sneer; "at Vilvoorden* she'll find six or seven hundred of her
cousins!"

"But how is it possible?" said an old chair-
mender, with a sigh. "I would have trusted Jan-
Grap with my last stiver."

"Such good, upright people, who never did anybody an injury!" added another.

"Who cared so little for money that they were
always giving alms, though they were not over
well off themselves."

"The most amiable, the best lad on the face of
the earth!"

"So merry and so clever! and *they* to rob like
this—to break into a house in the night."

"Yes," remarked the tailor's wife, "after this
nobody will be able to trust his own brother;
every thing that goes on two legs is a thief. So
much the worse for them that let themselves be
caught."

"Come, come, Betty," said a mason; laughingly, "'tisn't quite so bad as that comes to, either.
Because your husband cabbages a bit of cloth now

---

* A prison at Antwerp.

and then, you think there are no honest people left."

"Ha! you've cheated the gallows," snarled the tailor's wife. "You've got the mark of 'em on you, you rogue!"

"Thank you very much, Betty darling!" said the mason, with a smile and a bow.

"Serves her right!" interposed the fish-wife. "I-don't like looking on at other people's troubles; but if *my lady* the schouwveger's wife is to figure on the scaffold, I'd be off to the great market, if I was on my deathbed."

"Fie, you shrew!" exclaimed one of the girls. "I can't think how you can take pleasure in the misfortunes of your neighbors. What good will it do you, now, if the Smets are sent to prison?"

"You simpleton!" said the fish-wife, with a smile of contempt; "you would rather see thieves running about at large, I suppose?"

The girl was about to reply; but at this moment an old dame thrust her head into the circle, and said—

"But, bless my soul! do you know how Jan-Grap did the job?"

Every one looked at her with intense curiosity.

"Only think!" she continued. "Never trust anybody again as long as you live! I've always said, and I maintain the same now, that the law ought to prevent so much gold money being put in the windows before people's eyes. Yes, when a poor body is standing at a money-changer's shop, and his eyes fall on the heaps of gold-pieces, 'tis just as if the devil was tempting him. I'm old now; but, for all that, whenever I pass a money-changer's, and the gold twinkles before my eyes, then my heart begins to beat terribly, and I'm all of a shake with longing; you wouldn't believe, now, that I'm quite afraid to trust myself. There's Trees, the dustman's wife, who is always standing staring into the windows; only yesterday I said to her, 'Well done, Trees; that's the way to the gallows!'"

"Yes, yes, to be sure," remarked the chair-mender; "more than one have been made villains of, only by the sight of money."

"When you have seven children in your house, all shaking and shivering with hunger and cold," grumbled a mechanic, "and you see great heaps of gold lying there doing nothing, and think that one little piece would make you and your children so happy, it is indeed enough to make a man forget himself."

"But, Mother Beth, go on with your story about Master Smet!" was the universal cry.

"Ha, yes; well, it was like this. Poor Jan-Grap had got the bad habit of standing at the money-changer's window, to look at the piles of gold-pieces. Eight or ten days ago he was sent for to sweep a chimney; it was at a money-changer's, and there he saw heaps of gold. That very night he broke open the money-changer's door, and stole as much gold as he could carry."

"What a thief!" said the tailor, with a sigh.

"He managed uncommonly well," continued the old dame; "and never a crow would have cawed about it, if his stupid wife, with her airs and her finery, had not let it all out."

"Now, do you know whom I pity most?" said a girl: "'tis Katie, the shoemaker's daughter. Look at her, standing there, poor creature; she is half dead with grief."

"I can well believe that," was the reply. "Dame Smet was always telling her that she should be a *my lady* too, and live in a big house on the Meir. She has turned the poor thing's head; and now all her castles in the air have tumbled to pieces. She was going to be married; now she'll have to wait ten or fifteen years, till her Pauw has served out his time at Vilvoorden."

"How can Pauw help it, if his father has done wrong?" stammered the girl.

"Yes, but you see," mumbled the old dame, "the footprints in the money-changer's house show that the schouwveger was not alone."

"Poor Pauw! poor Katie!" said the girl, with a melancholy voice, as if oppressed by a painful conviction.

"The gendarmes won't catch Pauw," said one. "He's a slippery rogue; he's made himself scarce betimes. He's over the frontier by this time, you may be sure, with his pockets well lined."

"Kobe, you spit-venom!" exclaimed the mechanic. "I saw Pauw on the ramparts only a

minute or two ago. He was running up and
down like a body who has lost his senses."

"Don't you see, he knows all about it? If a
man isn't guilty, he has no cause for fear."

"No; I suppose you wouldn't have him laugh
when the gendarmes came to seize his father and
mother!"

No one had any doubt of the schouwveger's
guilt; most of the neighbors even felt a secret joy
at the disgrace which had fallen on his supercilious
wife.

Yet many stood there with sadness on their
countenances and in their hearts, and really
mourned over the fate of Master Smet and his ·
son. The whole affair to them was a mystery.
Such fine fellows, beloved by everybody for their
good-humor and kindness—that *they* should have
perpetrated a robbery at dead of night! Jan-
Grap and Pauwken-Plezier, who seemed to live
in such full trust in God's providence and grace—
that *they* should have committed · so horrible a
crime—for lust of gold!

But, though these friends of the schouwveger's
tried very hard to find arguments to vindicate him
in their own minds, the sight of the gendarme,
who stood at the door, overthrew them all at once.

The schouwveger was all this time sitting in the
front room of his house. He was quite prostrated,
and had buried his head · in his hands. An
officer kept watch over him while his wife was
being examined in the back room.

In this room there were assembled two or three personages of the supreme court of judicature, and in addition, the commissary of police and two gendarmes. They had made Dame Smet sit down opposite the judge who was to interrogate her. She smiled with wonderful boldness, and did not appear in the least disconcerted.

"You say," continued the judge, "that you have had the money in your house a long time, and that it is a part of your father's inheritance?"

"Yes."

"Yet it is notorious that your father left no money of any kind behind him."

"I suppose I know best about that," replied the dame, without hesitation. "What he gave me during his illness would not, of course, be found after his death."

"And to how much, now, did the money amount that you have kept concealed hitherto?"

The dame seemed to reflect a moment.

"Come, now, speak; if you don't know the exact sum, how much was it—about, as near as you can guess?"

"I see clearly," said Dame Smet, with a smile, "you are trying to catch me with some trick or other; but it won't do, gentlemen; I am not to be caught so easily."

"How much?" said the judge, with an accent of command.

"It might be a few thousand crowns."

"But how many thousand?"

"I don't know exactly; I haven't written it in any book."

"Was it ten thousand?"

"Yes, more than that."

"But how can you explain that you have lived here for twenty years as poor working-people; and now, all at once, you run about from shop to shop with your pockets full of gold? Here are hundreds of crowns spent in clothes and jewels; and now you are trying to get a house that would stand you in at least four thousand francs a year."

"Everybody has his own tastes. I am of a good family, and I expected that I should soon have a legacy from *my aunt* in Holland, who is enormously rich. So I said to myself, 'I will save up my money till I can begin to live in a style suitable to my rank.'"

"How much money have you in the house now?"

"No more."

"How, no more? Yesterday you showed a whole handful of gold-pieces to the owner of a house on the St. James's market. What has become of that money?"

"Suppose I chose to give it away, and didn't wish to say to whom?"

The judge shook his head angrily, and said—

"You are making up a story, and not telling the truth. We'll find a way to bring you to your senses. Your husband is now going to appear before us. Take notice, that if you speak a single

word until I ask you a question, you shall be taken
out into the other room."

Then, turning to a gendarme, he said—

"Bring the husband here."

When the schouwveger entered the room and
saw the judges of the supreme court there, he
began to tremble so violently that the gendarme
was obliged to support him to the chair which had
been placed for him. He was bloodless as a corpse,
and did not seem to hear the first questions of the
judge.

They gave him a little time to recover himself,
and in the meanwhile the examiners interchanged
significant looks with one another, as though the
mortal terror of the suspected man convinced them
that they had the real criminal before them.

What most disconcerted the schouwveger was
the sight of his wife, who seemed wonderfully cool,
but kept her eye fixed on that of her husband with
a penetrating severity of expression.

Master Smet had resolved to tell the whole truth;
but now that his wife held him fascinated by the
expression of her eye, his courage quite forsook
him.

"Now, answer me," said the judge to him at
length; "where does the money come from that
we find all at once in your possession?"

"My wife—my wife has inherited it," said
the schouwveger, with a confused and stammering
voice.

"From her aunt in Holland, isn't it?

"Yes, I believe so."

Dame Smet became livid with repressed wrath; she shook with the violence of the efforts she made to restrain herself, but it was all in vain. She exclaimed, with angry impetuosity—

"Confound you! what are you prating about there?—He has had a blow on the head, gentlemen; he has no more sense than a baby six weeks old. What use is it to ask questions of such a poor simpleton?"

"Gendarme," said the judge, authoritatively, "take the wife by the arm; at the least word or sign lead her off!"

Dame Smet trembled with rage, yet she did not dare to speak again. It was probably not without design that they kept her in the room; for the examiners carefully took notice of all the changing emotions which depicted themselves on her countenance.

"You say, then," asked the judge, turning to the schouwveger, "that your wife has inherited some money from her aunt in Holland?"

"Yes—no, no—from her father—rest his soul!" was the feeble and reluctant answer.

"Yes and no? Take care, my man; don't play your jokes with the law. You may have cause to rue it. Now tell me plainly and without circumlocution,—where does the money come from?"

Master Smet returned no answer. The examiners thought that his silence was intentional, but they were wrong. The poor man was quite paralyzed by terror; he could not speak.

"Is it always thus," continued the judge, "that you have accounted to the neighbors for your sudden wealth? Have you not spoken of a sum of money which you had borrowed in advance, on the security of your expected legacy?"

"Oh, sir," sighed Master Smet, rubbing his pale forehead, "I don't know. Yes, I believe it was so."

A peculiar expression of contemptuous compassion passed over the features of the examiners.

"And the money you borrowed amounted to a considerable sum? some thousand crowns?"

"No, no—a few hundreds."

"Not thousands, then?"

"I don't know clearly."

"Speak the truth," exclaimed the judge, raising his voice, and using a gesture of threatening; "we know all about it. Your wife is better advised than you are. She maintains that you have borrowed several thousand crowns."

A fresh nervous paroxysm shook the poor schouwveger.

"It is possible," he faltered out; "I don't know what I am saying. Yes—some thousands—"

The judge allowed a few moments to elapse, and then addressed him with a voice of reassuring kindness:

. "My man, you are not straightforward, and you

are contradicting yourself at every word you say.
I will tell you what you are accused of; perhaps
you may then see that you have nothing to gain
by concealing the truth from us.   About ten days
ago, on a Friday night, a considerable quantity of
gold and silver was stolen from a money-changer's.
You are suspected of being the thief; and all the
circumstances, your own words themselves, witness
against you.   If you don't wish to be led off to
prison by the gendarmes, tell me, at once and
truly, where the money came from that has been
seen in your wife's possession."

The schouwveger stared at the judge, quite
bewildered, and unable to utter a word.

"You admit, then," asked the judge, "that
you are guilty, and that you have committed this
crime ?"

"No, no," exclaimed the terrified man; "I have
not stolen—"

"Can you explain to us why, on that very night,
you roused the neighbors by your cries for help?
why you shouted, 'Fire, fire!'?   Was it not in order
to make them believe that you had been all night
in your own house, and thus to conceal your
criminal visit to the money-changer from the eyes
of justice ?"

"I had been dreaming," sighed the schouwveger,
with a scarcely audible voice ; and then his head
sank down on his breast as though he had been
stunned by a sudden blow.

"We know enough," said the judge, rising;

"we shall obtain further evidence by searching the premises."

He gave the signal, and Master Smet and his wife were seized by the gendarmes; and all who were present followed the judge.

The terrified husband and wife were led all over the house; every thing was thrown into confusion, not the smallest corner remaining unexplored.

Dame Smet was quite unconcerned, and smiled, from time to time, at the fruitlessness of the search. She looked her husband full in the face at intervals, and seemed thus at once to encourage him to stand firm, and to threaten him if he lost his presence of mind.

In the attic several planks were taken up; for the plaster with which the rat-holes had been stopped excited suspicion. But they found nothing.

The judge asked many questions about the gold that had so mysteriously disappeared, but he could not extract from Dame Smet any sufficient explanation. The schouwveger leaned, almost insensible, against the wall, and could give no answer. He gazed at the beam like a man petrified; his treasure was there!

Amazed and vexed at his fruitless efforts to discover the stolen money, the judge abandoned the search and slowly descended the stairs.

Smet and his wife were again brought into the room, and there the gendarmes produced their ropes and handcuffs, at a sign given them by the judge. When the schouwveger saw these degrading preparations, he uttered a mournful shriek, and fell fainting on a chair.

His wife, on the contrary, regarded these preliminaries with a smile of disdain, as though she thought them but a feint to shake their courage.

"For the last time," said the judge, in a severe tone of voice; "there are the cords with which your hands will be tied behind your back. You will be led as a criminal through the streets to the prison. For the last time I beg you, for your own sake, to speak the truth. Where did all your money come from?"

The schouwveger was half dead with terror and apprehension; the perspiration stood in large drops on his forehead; and, as though his fear had deprived him of speech, he stared unconsciously at the floor.

'Well, now, speak; where did the money come from?"

A mournful scream echoed at this moment from the front room, and, before the judge could finish his question, a young man sprang shrieking into the apartment. He looked round with a glance rapid as lightning; and he must have heard the question of the judge, for he fell on his knees before the schouwveger, and, lifting his hands with a gesture of earnest entreaty, he cried—

"Oh, father, father! where did the money come from? Oh, for God's sake, speak! *You* steal? *you* a villain? Gendarmes, cords, handcuffs! No, no, it is impossible! it is a hideous dream!

The deadly paleness of the youth, his hair standing erect with fright, and the unutterably powerful appeal that lay in the glance of his eyes, made so deep an impression on the schouwveger that he burst into a flood of tears, and exclaimed, with a tremulous voice—

"I have deserved it all!   God has punished me!"

"Deserved? deserved?" yelled Pauw, tearing his hair in an agony.

But Master Smet drew himself up, wiped away the tears from his eyes, and raising his son from the ground, he pressed him to his heart with eager affection, saying, in a cheerful tone—

"No, my child, your father has done very wrong; but he is an honest man; he will explain all."

And turning himself to the judge, he said, with calm deliberation—

"Sir, I will show you the treasure, and you shall see how the money came into our hands."

Dame Smet thrust her fists into his face threateningly, and roared, with her features convulsed by passion—

"If you dare, coward!"

"Gendarme, lead the wife away!" said the judge.

"There is no need, sir," said the schouwveger; "my resolution is taken; I will explain every thing to you as I ought to have done at first. I have not stolen; it is a treasure I have found."

Pauw fell on his knees in the middle of the room, and exclaimed, with tears of joy and gratitude—

T

"Oh, my God, I thank thee, I thank thee for thy mercy and goodness!"

"Are you now ready to give us a full explanation?" asked the judge.

"Yes, yes," replied the schouwveger; "but, sir, I have a request to make. Will you have the goodness to grant it?"

"We shall see; if it is possible."

"You see, sir, this money has made me miserable; it is the pest of my house. Oh, have compassion on me, and take this plague away! take it all away with you!"

Dame Smet began to sob and cry aloud.

"Well, show us the treasure," said the judge, with a voice of authority.

The schouwveger led the officers of justice up to the attic, showed him that the great beam was hollow at the bottom, and said—

"The gold is in there. Ten days ago, one Friday evening, the rats were scampering about the attic and making a terrible noise; I was chasing two of them with an old sabre that is now hanging behind my bed. By chance I struck this beam, and was astonished at the hollow sound it gave; at the second blow, a square plank and a bag of money fell out on my toes. I have nothing else to say, gentlemen, except that the fear of thieves, and the fear that you would take away the money from us, have made me say and do a great many foolish and wicked things. This, you see, is the pure and simple truth."

And with these words he took the plank out of
the beam, and showed the judge the cavity.

The judge stooped and drew out the bag of
money; a large number of gold and silver pieces
rolled out on the floor, because the bag, rotten
with age, had burst a second time. But, at the
same time, there fell from the beam something
else, which the schouwveger had not noticed. It
was a small, well-worn pocketbook, with a parch-
ment cover.

Conjecturing that this book might contain a
confirmation or a refutation of the explanation
made by the schouwveger, the judge seized it
eagerly, and turned it over with very remarkable
attention.

Turning to the weeping Dame Smet, he asked—

"What is your father's name, my woman?"

"Vandenberg, Peter Vandenberg," sobbed she.

Without further remark the judge ripped up the
bag still wider, and gathered out of it a certain
number of pieces. Then he made a sign to his
companions, and, drawing them aside in a corner,
he said to them—

"This man speaks the truth; there are no crimi-
nals here. This little book is a memorandum-
book of the wife's father, telling the sums of money which he had deposited, from time to time, in
the beam; and he has even written in it that he
destined the whole of it to his daughter. We
know the man had the reputation of being miserly
and rich; and as he died suddenly, he had no time

to say where his money was hidden. Besides, look, the treasure contains old ducats, French crowns, and even Brabant shillings. It is not money like this that the money-changer has been robbed of. We have nothing further to do here."

His hearers nodded their heads approvingly.

Then going up to the schouwveger, the judge said—

"My man, you have given yourself a great deal of unnecessary trouble and vexation. The money is legally yours."

"Oh, take it away with you!" implored Master Smet.

"Simpleton!" said the judge, with a smile; "we have nothing to do with it. Listen; the seven hundred and sixteenth article of the city statute-book says: 'The right of property in a treasure belongs to him who finds it on his own premises; if he finds it on any other man's premises, then half belongs to the finder and half to him on whose premises it is found!' This house is yours; consequently, the whole treasure belongs to you."

"Then the plague must remain in my house!" muttered the schouwveger, discontentedly.

To Dame Smet, who came rushing forward with joy and eagerness, the judge said—

"Dame, this gold is the inheritance your father has bequeathed you; you must regard this little book as his will. Farewell, and try both of you to make a good use of your riches."

While the officers of justice were leaving the attic, the dame was gathering the money, in speech-less haste, into her apron, and then she ran down-stairs with it, snarling the while at her husband—

"Coward! confound you! I'll pay you out for this!"

When she had brought all her treasure down-stairs, she threw it in the chest, took out a hand-ful of gold-pieces, locked the chest, and then ran out into the street, and strutted with haughty ex-ultation through the assembled crowd, who stood gaping and staring after her until she had disap-peared from the little street.

Pauw was quite wild with joy. He rushed down the stairs to go to Katie; but, seeing the shoe-maker and his daughter in the street, he seized a hand of each, and cried—

"Ha, come, come, Katie dear, it was all moon-shine! Master Dries, come with me; my father will be so happy if you come and wish him luck."

Already the result of the search was known to the waiting crowd.

"Pauw, Pauw, good luck, *Mynheer* Pauw!" shouted the young girls, clapping their hands with sincere and hearty congratulations.

"Oh, call me always Pauwken-Plezier!" said the young man, imploringly, as he led the shoe-maker and his daughter toward the door.

"Long live Pauwken! Long live Pauwken-Plezier!" resounded through the street.

The schouwveger no sooner saw his friend the

shoemaker than he burst into tears, and rushed to meet him with open arms. Pressing his old friend to his heart, he sobbed aloud—

"Oh, Dries, look, this is the happiest day of my life! I totter on my legs with joy. What I have suffered from this cursed money passes all description; no pen could write it!"

"Is every thing all clear now?" asked the shoemaker.

"Yes, yes; we found the gold here in the house; it was the inheritance of my wife."

"God be praised, Jan! I have been sitting shaking all over as if you were my own brother."

"Well, Dries, you are all the same as my own brother. Listen; now we'll make haste, and let our children be married."

"But you are a rich man now? Your wife?" muttered the shoemaker.

"What do you mean by rich?" said Master Smet, merrily. "I am still Jan-Grap, your friend. We've sung out our song about *my ladies* and *mamsels!* Now that I don't mean to bother myself about the money, I'll soon see whether I'm master or not!"

"I ask nothing better than to see my child happy," answered his friend. "Not for the money; but they have loved one another, with a virtuous love and with our approbation, many a long year. My poor Katie—I believe she would have wasted away, really, in case—"

"Come, come, not a word more about such

horrid things as that!" exclaimed the schouwveger. "Let me see: drawing up the papers;
the banns in church;—yes, within seven weeks
we'll have the wedding-feast! Ha, that shall be
a feast, friend Dries! That shall be something to
talk about! Money shall be of some use for once.
I'll invite all the neighbors, and we'll set off in
five or six coaches to Dikke-Mê or to Jan-Stèk's.*
We'll take the fiddlers with us, and we'll dance
and *flikker*, we'll sing and jump—bless me! won't
we, then?"

His voice failed him, and he burst suddenly into
tears.

"What is the matter, Jan?" asked the astonished shoemaker.

"Nothing; 'tis nothing at all, my friend," faltered
out the schouwveger; "only my gladness sticks
in my throat. My heart is full—running over. I
have gone through so much these last few days,
that I seem now as if I had escaped out of hell!"

With increasing emotion, he continued—

"That's settled, isn't it, Dries?—our children are
to be married as soon as possible, without a single
day's delay?"

"'Tis rather soon, isn't it?"

"Good things are never too soon: this cursed
money may come in the way again. But, Dries,
I've one thing to ask of you. You see, your tem-

---

* Two large taverns outside the city of Antwerp, favorite
resorts of the citizens.

per is rather short, and my wife's tongue is rather
long; now, these two things don't get on well
together.   She will be sure to show her teeth
when she sees you, for she fancies it is all your
doing that the officers of justice paid us a visit.
You're looking rather sour about it.   Now, keep
your temper, man, and be reasonable; and a little
accommodating, too.   My wife may be uncivil to
you : well, let her have her way.   We have the
disposal of our children, anyhow; and if we make
up our minds that they shall be married, who is
to hinder it ?"

"That is true."

"Well, now, you won't be put out by a few
words and ugly faces, will you ?"

"No; I'll act as if I were blind and deaf."

" Come, now, that's spoken like a sensible man.
Give me your hand; that's settled, then.

He turned then to his son and Katie, who were
standing at the window, clasping each other's
hands, and had probably heard all that had been
said; for their countenances beamed with radiant
joy, though quiet tears were trickling down their
cheeks.

"Come, Katie," cried the schouwveger, "hug
me round the neck, girl; seven weeks more and
I shall be your father!"

The girl ran, with an exclamation of heartfelt
gladness, and threw her arms round the schouwveger's neck.   Pauw had rushed toward his
father under the impulse of a similar emotion;

and all four were rapt in the bliss of true, sincere, heartfelt affection.

"Eh! eh! what's this going on in my house?" resounded all at once through the room, in a threatening tone.

As though this voice had thrilled painfully to their hearts, they released themselves from each other's arms, and looked with astonishment toward the door.

There stood Dame Smet, tossing her head in the air, and with a smile of ineffable contempt on her face.

"Well, well, these are pretty doings!" exclaimed she; "I can't leave the house a minute but when I come back I find it full of cobblers!"

The shoemaker's face became pale with rage.

"Yes, yes; be as sulky as you like," said she, with an expression of scornful disdain; "I shall only laugh at you for your pains. I am mistress here."

"But, Dame Smet—" stammered the shoemaker.

"Dame! dame! I am no *dame*," snarled she; "you must say *my lady*, when you presume to speak to me!"

Pauw looked steadily at his father, for he saw that he was quivering with anger and vexation.

Dame Smet pointed to the door, and said to the shoemaker, in a tone of great excitement—

"Be off! quick! out of my house with your dainty daughter! That such mean, vulgar people should ever cross my threshold, indeed! 'Tis a

good thing that we are going to live on the St.
James's market, with a *porte-cochère* all to ourselves!"

The shoemaker took his daughter's hand, and
led her out into the street, muttering to himself
as he went.

Then burst forth the schouwveger's wrath in an
impetuous and irresistible storm. He uttered un-
intelligible sounds; he sprang at his wife—but
Pauw had placed himself between them, and kept
them apart with desperate effort.

"Let me go! let me go!" yelled Master Smet.
"I'll twist her haughty neck for her."

Pauw prayed, and implored, and shed tears, and
made such successful resistance, that his father had
time to recover himself and cool down a little.

After a few more threats and execrations, the
schouwveger said, as if quite overcome—

"Come, Pauw, come up-stairs, or that woman
will give me a fit of apoplexy." And, according
to his wont, he ran quickly up the stairs to avoid
further altercation.

The whole day was spent thus in quarrelling
and in sullenness. The dame declared she would
not hear Katie's name mentioned, and poured out
a flood of abuse against the poor girl and her
father.

Now she had the notion of some *my lady* more
firmly fixed in her head than before. Leocadie, at
the corner shop, had already become far too vulgar
to be admitted into *her* family.

Pauw did nothing but weep, and retired into his room very early, to bewail his wretched fate in solitude.

At length the schouwveger went slowly up-stairs, muttering, in the bitterness of his soul—

"The plague is still in my house, I see! This cursed money! I wish it would sink down through the earth into the pit it came from!"

CHAPTER VIII.

VERY early the next morning, when the first beams of the sun were beginning to disperse the gloom of the little street, the shoemaker and his daughter were on their way to church; but they had scarcely left their door, and walked a few steps down the street, when the girl suddenly stood still, and said, pointing to the schouwveger's house—

"Father, look! Master Smet's door is wide open; the windows are all bolted still!"

"Good heavens! what can it be?" exclaimed the shoemaker. "The lock is wrenched off the door. Depend on it, the thieves have been there to-night. Come, Katie, I will knock them up."

And so saying, he began to kick at the door to awaken the inmates of the house.

"Don't kick so hard, father," said the girl,

trembling with apprehension; "you'll frighten Dame Smet. Wait a bit; give them time to get their clothes on."

After a short pause, the shoemaker began to kick again; and when he heard, a few moments after, the sound of footsteps on the stairs, he entered the house.

"Who opened the door to you?" asked Dame Smet, in a menacing tone. "Didn't I tell you you were to keep away from my house?"

"There you are at it again!" growled the schouwveger. "Pauw has gone to the first mass, I suppose. But, anyhow, Master Dries can't have dropped through the ceiling."

"No, no, my friends, it is not as you think," said the shoemaker; "your door has been broken open. I am quite in a fright; I am afraid something has happened."

"The door broken open!" shrieked Dame Smet, while a mortal paleness overspread her face; "oh, my money, my money!"

She ran with an eager cry to the chest, and threw it open. A stifled groan broke from her breast; she covered her face with her hands, and fell on a chair, sobbing in anguish and despair.

"My money—my money is gone!" she cried "stolen—stolen!"

The schouwveger seemed surprised at the un expected tidings, and remained a moment staring round, as though he were asking whether he ought to laugh or cry. But in a moment his mind reco-

vered itself; a smile ran over his features, but he
forcibly repressed this indication of gladness; and,
that he might not add to his wife's distress, he
behaved as if he were quite amazed—yes, even
somewhat afflicted.

Katie had taken Dame Smet's hand, and was
crying with sincere sympathy.

"Jan," said the shoemaker, in a soothing tone,
"'tis a great misfortune, my friend; but you must
not be crushed down. by it. 'God giveth—God
taketh away. I am very sorry for your distress."

"My distress!" said Master Smet, speaking in
a low voice, that his wife might not overhear him;
"if you fancy I'm going to shed one tear for this
bewitched money that was doomed to make me
wretched, you are much mistaken, friend Dries.
I am sorry for my wife; but for that I should
say—'God be praised that the plague is well out
of my house!'"

"Oh, oh!" groaned Dame Smet, wringing her
hands, "my money—my poor money! the legacy
of my father! 'Twill be the death of me."

And indeed the poor woman looked so dread-
fully ill, that the schouwveger feared she was going to faint away, and, running for some vinegar,
he poured out a handful, and rubbed it on the face
of his wife; but she repelled him angrily, as
though she would not be tended by him.

"Let me alone!" she cried, snappishly. "You
are in high feather about it; I see it clear enough
on your hypocritical face!"

"Come, now, Trees," said he, "you mustn't take on so about it. The money is gone, sure enough; but our miserable life, our quarrels, and all our vexations and grievances, are gone away with it too. Come, come, dame, pluck up your courage. I shall set to work again briskly enough. We shall live in peace, and our days will glide away merrily, just as they used to do." .

"Oh, mother, mother!" cried Katie, "how unfortunate you are!"

"Yes," sobbed the dame; "you, only you, child, have any sympathy with me. The unfeeling log of wood! there he stands grinning in my face! He'd see anybody die before his very eyes, without giving them a single word of comfort. I feel grateful to you, Katie, for crying with me. Oh, oh! my money, my money!

At this moment Pauw came running down the stairs.

"Eh! eh! what's up now?" said he, with a laugh. "I begin to believe that our house is bewitched. And Katie, *you* here? with my mother? Ha, ha! then you've made it all up?"

"Be quiet, Pauw," said the schouwveger; "a great misfortune has happened. The thieves have stolen all our money in the night!"

"Well, thank God! thank God!" shouted Pauw, cutting an unusually vigorous *flikker;* "that's capital! Now, Pauwken-Plezier will be a schouwveger again!"

His mother, deeply wounded by his unfeeling

rapture, sprang to her feet, and exclaimed, angrily—

"You, too, you good-for-nothing boy, *you* laugh
at my distress!"

The young man took her hand, and murmured,
in a tone of sympathy and affection, as though
he had now first grasped the real state of the
case—

"Oh, mother, I never thought of that; you have
been crying! indeed, indeed, you must be in great
distress."

And he led her gently back to her chair, sat
down by her side, and, pressing her hand tenderly,
he said—

"Mother dear, look up a bit. The loss of the
money must be a great trouble to you—I quite feel
that; but think, now, that we were not happy with
it. Since it came into our possession, there have
been more irritation, more quarrelling, more vexa
tion, in our house than in all my life before. You
and father—you used to be so affectionate to each
other, and every thing was so comfortable and so
nice, that one couldn't be better off in the king's
palace. From the day the money was found, you
have been always sad, and always looking as sour
as vinegar; father has been growing thin, Katie
has been pining away, and I was losing my wits
fast. There was nothing but suffering and annoyance!"

"Yes, Pauw, but it was all your father's fault,"
answered the dame; "he couldn't bear his sudden

wealth; but I, who am of a good family, I was born to be rich, you see."

"Yes, everybody knows that well," said Pauw, with a gentle, insinuating voice; "but you are my mother for all that, and you have no other child but me. And since you know now that the money made father and me miserable, you, who are so tender and loving, won't you take a little comfort? Won't you say to yourself: 'In God's name, then, 'tis all the same if only we are peaceful and contented'?"

"To be poor—*poor!*" said Dame Smet, sobbing afresh.

"Come, Trees, be a reasonable woman!" said the schouwveger; "isn't affection worth more than any thing else? We have lived so long together, and we have loved each other so truly—so we will again; and perhaps hereafter you will bless God that he has taken the wretched money from us."

"Hold your tongue," snarled she; "I dare say you have been praying for this."

"But, mother," continued Pauw, "only think a bit how things were before. Father and I—we were always full of mirth; we had always something funny to make people laugh; everybody loved us. There was never a cross word in the house, or in the street, or in the whole neighborhood; everybody was a friend to us."

He threw his arms round her neck, and murmured, with thrilling tenderness in his voice—

"Look, mother, this beautiful and happy life

will come back again; father and I will drink a
pint of beer the less, and save to buy you a fine
dress now and then; and as Katie will live with
you, you will be waited on like a *my lady;* we
shall love you, and treat you with respect. You
will have more happiness and enjoyment in your
life than you would have with the money."

"But, Pauw, lad, what will people say when
I pass along the street?" said Dame Smet, with a
melancholy voice.

"What will they say? Oh, mother, I'll go with
you and father this very day, and will have a walk
on the Dyke. I'll walk by your side, and give you
my arm; I'll carry my head up, and look everybody full in the face. We are honest people.
Those who don't know us won't care about us, and
those who do will say that we are sensible, strong-
minded people, who take thankfully either fortune
or misfortune, as it pleases God to send it."

The half-consoled dame began to weep afresh.
She pressed her son to her heart, and said—

"In God's name, then, I shall be a rich woman
some day; if not now, then it will be hereafter.
You must be a schouwveger again, then, Pauw.
It frets me; but as it cannot be otherwise, and
since you like it—"

She then released Pauw, and bestowed a similar
embrace on the girl at her side.

"Come, Katie, darling child, you are the best
of them all," sobbed she. "Men don't know
what it is to be rich; but you would soon have got

U

used to it, wouldn't you? Well, 'twill come some day. Don't fret about it. *My aunt* in Holland can't last much longer; she must be more than eighty years old."

Pauw had silently left the room without being observed.

Suddenly, as though a terrible thought had pierced her heart, Dame Smet began to tremble; she sprang up, and, stretching out her hands toward her husband, she exclaimed—

"Oh, good heavens! Smet, there's five-and-twenty crowns to be paid at the jeweller's. Oh, my God, what a debt! We shall never be able to pay it! To be poor isn't so bad—but to be in debt!"

And with a lamentable voice, she added, "There is one way—'tis very hard, but any thing rather than debt—I'll take my jewels back to him."

The schouwveger pressed her hand, and said, cheerfully—

"No, no, Trees dear, you shall not take any thing back; you may keep all you have got."

"But who will pay for them?"

"I will, I will, Trees."

"You?"

"Yes; I had put a little money on one side, to provide against accidents, and for Pauw's wedding. Wait a moment!"

He placed a chair on the hearth, thrust his head up the chimney, reached out a piece of cloth in which he had wrapped the money, and then he went to the table, and spread out a number of gold-pieces on it.

Dame Smet was deeply affected by the sight of this little remnant of her legacy. A glad smile played on her features; her bosom heaved; and she gazed without speaking on the glittering gold.

"Look you, Trees," said her husband, "this money belongs to you; you may do what you like with it; only, I beg you, let us keep the greater part of it for Pauw and Katie's wedding, and to set them up in a little shop."

His wife said nothing, and seemed lost in deep thought.

Suddenly their attention was arrested by the cry—*aep, aep, aep!* which seemed to come from the cellar; and they all turned their eyes in that direction with a smile, for they had no doubt that it was Pauw's voice.

And in a moment he was heard singing, as lively and merry as ever—

> "Schouwvegers gay, who live in A. B.,
> Companions so jolly,
> All frolic and folly—"

and he came bounding into the room, making the most surprising gestures and grimaces.

He had put on all his chimney-sweeper's clothes, flourished his brush in his hand, and had blackened his face with soot.

"Hurrah!" shouted he; "Pauwken-Plezier's

U

come again! Father, mother, Katie, I'm *so* happy
Let us all be merry again! Sorrow and spleen are
afraid of a black face! Come, sing, dance, and
mirth forever!"

Pauw took Katie's hand, and proceeded to dance
round the room with her; but the girl resisted his
affectionate violence.

When he saw the chimney-sweeper's clothes
which he had worn from a child, and in which he
had enjoyed so much peace and pure joy, Master
Smet was affected in a very extraordinary manner.
He burst into tears, and sobbed aloud with joyful
emotion.

"Well done, Pauw! Ha, that's right, lad!" he
shouted. "There's nothing can beat a schouwveger's life! If your mother will let me, I'll put
on my black clothes, too. Ay, ay, Pauw, mirth
forever! So be it!"

The mother made a sign to them to be quiet, as
though she had something weighty to say.

She then turned to the shoemaker; and, reaching
forth her hand to him, with a gentle smile, she
said—

"Master Dries, I was much vexed yesterday; I
was very uncivil to you, wasn't I? Will you
forgive me? Shall we all be friends again as we
were before?"

The shoemaker shook her hand with hearty good-
will.

"All is forgiven and forgotten," replied he, with
tears in his eyes. "We both of us limp a little

bit on the same leg—soon put out and soon cooled down again. We were never cut out for enemies —we've been playfellows and good neighbors from the cradle."

Dame Smet then turned to her son, and said, pointing to the table—

"Pauw, your father put by that money to set you up in a little shop; I give it all to you. Marry Katie as soon as you can; but, if you love me, live with me still. I shall love Katie, and I will teach her good manners against the time my legacy comes."

"We will live with you, mother; we will live all united until death shall divide us," said Pauw.

"Oh, yes, yes, you will be my good, kind mother!" sobbed the girl.

"Well, bless me! how is it possible?" exclaimed Dame Smet, in unaffected amazement; "to be poor and yet be so happy!"

"Are you happy, mother dear?" asked Pauw, with joyful tenderness.

"Yes, yes, child; laugh and dance away as much as you like."

"Come, come, then—let's have a real hearty schouwveger's song and dance," said the lad, wild with joy; "just a little rehearsal for the wedding, Katie dear; let's hear Pauwken-Plezier's last new song!"

He took his parents and the shoemaker and Katie by the hand, and in a moment they were all whirling and skipping round the room, while the

young schouwveger roused all the echoes of the
old street with his lusty song:

"Schouwvegers gay, who live in A. B
    Companions so jolly,
    All frolic and folly,—
Schouwvegers gay, who live in A. B.,
    Come out, and sing us a glee.

Your schouwveger gay is a right merry fellow;
    Though sooty his skin,
    The wit's all within.
    The blacker his phiz
    The blither he is.
      He climbs and he creeps—
      He brushes and sweeps—
      He sings and he leaps— .
At each chimney he drinks till he's mellow.
      Aep, aep, aep!
    Light-hearted and free—
    Always welcome is he!"

.THE END.

THE APOSTLESHIP OF PRAYER ASSOCIATION.

☞ Especial attention is respectfully solicited to the following Works, on the *Apostleship of Prayer.*

Published with the Approbation of the Most Rev. ABP. SPALDING.

Just Published, in a neat volume, 12o., *cloth, price* $1. 50.

The Apostleship of Prayer. A Holy League of Christian Hearts united with the Heart of Jesus, to obtain the Triumph of the Church and the Salvation of Souls. Preceded by a Brief of the Sovereign Pontiff Pius IX, the Approbation of several Archbishops and Bishops, and Superiors of Religious Congregations. By the Rev. H. RAMIERE, of the Society of Jesus. Translated from the latest French Edition, and Revised by a Father of the Society.

Just Published, in a neat volume, 32o., *cloth, price* 40 cts.

The Manual of the Apostleship of Prayer. Enriched with ample Indulgences by His Holiness Pius IX, and Approved of by a large number of Archbishops and Bishops, and Affiliated to the Association of the Sacred Heart, established in Rome, in the Church *della Pace.* By the Rev. H. RAMIERE, S. J., Director of the Association. Translated from the French.

The Apostleship of Prayer Association. Explanation and Practical Instruction by FATHER RAMIERE, S. J. Translated from the French by a Father of the Society. Price, 5 cts., per 100, $3.

The Rosary of the Apostleship, In small pamphlet form.

☞ The large and constantly increasing demand for these Works, is an evidence of their merits, and the great popularity of this Association.

Just Published, per dozen, 60 cents, *per* 100, $3.50, *net.*

Circles of the Living Rosary, Illustrated.

Published with the Approbation of the Most Rev. Archbishop SPALDING.

This is an entirely New Translation, conformable to the Brief of HIS HOLINESS, POPE GREGORY XVI, January 27, 1832, each Mystery is accompanied by the Instructions, Prayers, Meditations, and a List of all the Indulgences granted by the Sovereign Pontiffs, to this widespread Devotion. ☞ The Circles are beautifully Illustrated, and Printed on Fine Paper.

Recently Published, 32o., *cloth,* 50 cents; *in finer bindings, up to* $2.

The Month of Mary, for the Use of Ecclesiastics.

Translated from the French.

APPROBATION OF THE MOST REV. ABP. SPALDING.

WE *have examined, and* WE *cordially approve the publication, in an English translation, of the Month of Mary, for the use of Ecclesiastics, and* WE *recommend it to the Clergy and Seminaries of* OUR *Archdiocese.* M. J. SPALDING, *Abp. of Balt.*

This little Work, in honor of the "Immaculate Queen of the Clergy," has been already heralded by, at east, six editions in French. This first English Edition, is confidently recommended to the Ecclesiastics of this country.

Church Registers.—*Registers of Baptisms, Marriages, Confirmations, Interments. Registers of Pews.—Parish Records.*

☞ These Books are carefully prepared with Printed Headings, and conveniently arranged, for keeping Church Records, in such a manner as to save time and labor to the Pastor, and affording great facility for reference at all times.

The PEW BOOKS are admirably arranged for keeping the Accounts in the most simple manner, showing at a glance the state of the Pew-holder's account. They are put up in Books of 2, 3 and 400 pages, and can be ordered to correspond to the number of Pews in a Church—a page being appropriated to each Pew.

This series of six Books are printed on Fine Cap Paper. They are uniformly bound in Books of various sizes, and may be had separately or in sets, done up in neat Walnut Cases.

MURPHY & Co. *Publishers and Catholic Booksellers, Baltimore.*

New and Improved Editions of Highly Important Works.

LADY FULLERTON'S TALES.

A New and Uniform Edition, in 3 vols., 12o., cloth, $1.50. Cloth, gilt edges, &c., $2 per vol.

Lady Bird.   Ellen Middleton.   Grantley Manor.

No less accomplished as an authoress than pious and unostentatious in private life, Lady Fullerton gives her works a character of instructiveness and practical wisdom which we look for in vain in many of our professedly religious ta'es. The young of her sex will find in her pages entertainment of the highest order, interest, beauty of style, elegance of description, without a line to pamper the silly or romantic ideas that too often unfit them for real life. The signal success of her works, not only in England, but in America, and their translation on the Continent, are the best evidences of their decided merit.

Pauline Seward. A Tale of Real Life. By J. D. BRYANT, M. D.
Sixth Revised Edition. Two volumes in one. New Edition, 12o., cloth, $1.50. Cloth, gilt edges, $2.

"No prose writer of America has yet, to our knowledge, penned a more graceful or more un-affected tale than this."—*London Sun.*

The Genius of Christianity; or, the Spirit and Beauty
of the Christian Religion. By VISCOUNT DE CHATEAUBRIAND. With a Preface, Biographical Notice of the Author, and Critical and Explanatory Notes, by the Rev. C. I. White, D. D. Embellished with a fine Steel Portrait. 800 pages, large 12mo. Cloth, $2.25. Cloth, extra full gilt, $3.

The *Genius of Christianity* is now presented to the Public for the *first time* in a Complete English translation, accompanied with a Biographical Notice of the distinguished Author.
This work was originally published in France, more than fifty years ago, and it has been pronounced by the best critics one of the most eloquent, instructive, and interesting productions of which the literature of the 19th Century can boast.

Balmes on European Civilization. Protestantism and Catholi-
city compared in their Effects on the Civilization of Europe. By Rev. J. BALMES. 8o. cloth $3. Library style, $3.50.

"This Book, to be known, must be read, and we would recommend all who would possess one of the great Books which has appeared in our day, to lose no time in procuring it."—*Brownson.*

Life of St. Francis Xavier. Apostle of the Indies and Japan, from
the Italian of BARTOLI and MAFFEI, with a Preface, by the Rev. Father FABER. 12o. cloth, $1.75 Cloth, gilt edges, $2.25.

Life of St. Vincent de Paul. Founder of the Congregation of the
Mission, and of the Sisters of Charity. By M. COLLET. New Edition, fine paper, 12o. cloth, $1.00. Cloth, gilt edges, $1.50.

The Studies and Teachings of the Society of Jesus, at the
Time of its Suppression, 1750–1775. Translated from the French of the ABBE MAYNARD, Honorary Canon of the Pointers, &c. 12o. cl. $1.

Milner's End of Religious Controversy. In a Friendly Cor-
respondence, between a Religious Society of Protestants, and a Catholic Divine. By the Rt. Rev. JOHN MILNER, D. D. A New Edition, just published, in small 8o. Cloth, $1.

Catholic Tracts, for General Circulation. Price $5 per 100 net.

The "Catholic" Church, and the Roman Catholic Church. In a Friendly Correspondence, between a Catholic Priest, and an Episcopal Minister.

Faith, Hope, and Charity. The Substance of a Sermon. By Bishop BAINE.

MURPHY & Co. *Publishers and Catholic Booksellers, Baltimore.*

www.ingramcontent.com/pod-product-compliance
Lightning Source LLC
Chambersburg PA
CBHW032011060726
47497CB00017B/3089